"I don't understand..."

Tess looked up at detective Ryan Hill, who regarded her with such empathy that it crumbled what little control she had left and she swayed on her feet again. Only this time, he caught her elbows in his strong hands and held her steady.

"Is she...going to be okay?" she murmured, wiping away the tears.

"The doctor said he thinks there's a good chance she'll pull through."

"Has the driver come forward? Have you found him yet?"

"There are a thousand white vans in New Harbor, Miss Mays. Without a license plate..." Detective Hill's voice trailed off as he ran a hand through his black, glossy hair. "There's a whole lot you need to know."

Tess looked away from his gaze, staring at the bank of monitors, then at the face that was at once familiar and foreign—her twin sister. Her twin. All those years of loneliness and she'd had a twin the whole time....

ALICE SHARPE

MY SISTER, MYSELF

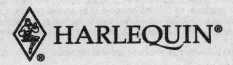

HARLEQUIN®

TORONTO • NEW YORK • LONDON
AMSTERDAM • PARIS • SYDNEY • HAMBURG
STOCKHOLM • ATHENS • TOKYO • MILAN • MADRID
PRAGUE • WARSAW • BUDAPEST • AUCKLAND

This book is dedicated to my sister, Mary Shumate.
Not a twin, but just as close to my heart.
I would like to thank Arnold Sharpe, Joseph Sharpe and
Jennifer Jones for their patience, support and expertise.
I love you all.

ISBN 0-373-88697-7

MY SISTER, MYSELF

ABOUT THE AUTHOR

Alice Sharpe met her husband-to-be on a cold, foggy beach in Northern California. One year later they were married. Their union has survived the rearing of two children, a handful of earthquakes registering over 6.5, numerous cats and a few special dogs, the latest of which is a yellow Lab named Annie Rose. Alice and her husband now live in a small rural town in Oregon, where she devotes the majority of her time to pursuing her second love, writing.

Alice loves to hear from readers. You can write her at P.O. Box 755, Brownsville, OR 97327. SASE for reply is appreciated.

Books by Alice Sharpe

HARLEQUIN INTRIGUE
746—FOR THE SAKE OF THEIR BABY
823—UNDERCOVER BABIES
923—MY SISTER, MYSELF*

*Dead Ringer

CAST OF CHARACTERS

Tess Mays—A fateful phone call disrupts her safe existence. Will she take up her long-lost twin sister's struggle to prove her dead father innocent?

Ryan Hill—A detective with the New Harbor police department, Ryan is committed to protecting both of his late partner's daughters. Trouble is, one is in a coma and the other is turning into a wonder woman right before his eyes.

Katie Fields—Tess's twin. What did she uncover before being struck down by a hit-and-run driver?

Matt Fields—His suspicious death in a house fire provides the catalyst that brings his long-separated daughters back together.

Caroline Mays—Tess and Katie's mother. But why did she keep her children apart and where is she now?

Nelson Lingford—What's the acute businessman's role in the fire that destroyed his stepmother's home?

Madeline Lingford—Would this crippled widow commit murder to protect her stepson?

Irene Woodall—The art dealer has obviously become Katie's confidant within the Lingford household. How can Tess circumnavigate her to get at the truth?

Vince Desota—His greed has all but destroyed his life, and he'll stop at nothing to get back at the man he blames for his failures.

Clint Doyle—A burly bodyguard who takes his job seriously. The question is: how seriously?

Jim Kinsey—A former Lingford employee, will he stop at nothing to get what he wants?

Georges—Irene's assistant. Why is he lying so low?

Prologue

Juggling an unwieldy umbrella and a cell phone, Katie Fields punched in the phone number, excitement turning to frustration as she reached Ryan's voice mail. She clicked off without leaving a message. Never mind. She'd catch up with him later and he'd be forced to eat crow as she provided proof that would clear her father's name.

Or would it?

The niggling voice in the back of her head, the voice she'd been trying her best to ignore, reminded her there was still the contents of that troubling suitcase to be explained.

She stared at the phone. She could make another call....

No. Not yet. That was the future, this was now.

Pocketing the phone, she hurried along

the slick sidewalk, struggling against the northwest wind and the wintry rain. Her car was just up ahead. She was so wrapped up in her battle with the elements that she didn't see or hear danger coming. It was only some sort of sixth sense that caused her to lower the umbrella at the last moment and face destruction head-on.

She screamed as she hit the wet sidewalk and then she knew nothing, nothing at all.

Chapter One

Tess took the taxi directly from the airport to the hospital, traveling the dark, rainy, unfamiliar streets in a state of numb distraction.

All she could hear in her head was the impersonal voice on the telephone telling her a fantastic story she still didn't believe. Well, she'd be at the hospital soon and then she'd know. Her stomach, which had been in a knot for hours now, clenched even tighter.

"This is it, lady," the cabbie said, rolling to a stop outside a huge, well-lit building. Gathering her duffel bag, Tess paid her fare before stepping outside into a puddle the size of a wading pool. Her San Francisco blood was too thin for this coastal Oregon chill, she thought, as she hugged her coat close and fought her way through the pelting rain into the hospital lobby.

She knew she needed to go up to the third floor. Once there, she found the ICU waiting room and activated the intercom. "I'm looking for Katie Fields," she said, saying the name aloud for the first time in her life. "I was told she's here."

"And you are?" the voice came back.

"Tess Mays. Theresa Mays. I believe I'm... expected."

Within a few moments she was standing outside the curtained cubicle and because she'd been hurrying ever since the startling call came hours before, she pushed aside the soft-blue drapes without pause, stopping only as they swished behind her.

There was one bed in the dimly lit room. One slight figure, still as death itself, occupied the bed. Lights blinked on the monitors. If there were accompanying sounds, Tess didn't hear them; blood rushing through her head obliterated everything but the wild thumping of her own heart.

She wasn't aware when she dropped her duffel bag to the floor or when her shoulder bag followed. Pushing damp hair behind her ears, she slowly moved toward the bed, nerves like fire ants skittering up and down her spine.

Tubes led from the patient's arm to an IV bag, her fingernails were torn and dozens of bloody scrapes crisscrossed her arms. As Tess's gaze made it to the woman's face, she paused, resting one hand on the guardrail as she peered down at the bruised and swollen features.

Familiar features.

It was true. Somehow, someway, she, a twenty-seven-year-old only child raised by a single mother eight hundred miles south of here, had acquired an unconscious identical twin sister.

Swaying, she clutched the side of the bed and murmured, "I don't understand...."

She heard her own whispered words and, just like that, the beeping of the machines and a sound came from the shadows. She looked up as a man materialized from the far corner. Taking a step back, she covered her mouth with one hand.

"You're Theresa Mays," he said, his face coming into the light. Tess stared at him as he stared at her, a stalemate of sorts. But the fact that he knew her name finally made an impact and she dropped her hand.

He wasn't a doctor, unless doctors at this hospital had adopted a dress code of jeans and black leather jackets, two-day-old beards and unruly jet-black hair. He appeared to be in his early thirties, a tall man with broad shoulders and features cut from a mountainside. The unsettled look on his face made Tess shudder. He held a rectangle of paper in his hand and he ran his fingers along the fold as he said, "I didn't really believe it until this moment. You look exactly like her."

"Who are you?" Tess said. "How do you know my name?"

"I've been expecting you," he said, walking around the bed, his gaze never leaving her face. He was a big man, and Tess was a small woman, something that hit home every time one of her larger patients got rambunctious, like the Newfoundland jokingly named Mouse who outweighed Tess and liked to sit on her feet.

It finally dawned on Tess that the strongest emotion emanating from this man was confusion.

Join the club....

He produced a badge. "My name is Ryan Hill. I'm a detective with the New Harbor police force."

With a glance back at the silent woman in

the bed, Tess said, "Is this about...her...accident?"

"I worked with her father. He was my partner. I take it you didn't know your father," he said gently.

Tess shook her head. He was using the past tense, but her brain kept coming up with explanations other than the obvious one.

"I think you should read this," Detective Hill said, stepping closer and handing Tess the paper. It was dog-eared and much folded as though read and reread a million times.

Tess took it almost reluctantly, unfolding it into a handwritten letter. She looked over at her unconscious sister again, then back at the letter, tilting it toward the light in order to see better.

My dear Katie,

If you're reading this, I'm dead. Of course, being in law enforcement all these years has put me in harm's way more often than most, so I guess it's not too big a surprise. I want you to know any mistakes I made were my own damn fault. That said, you need to know something, Katie, something I swore I would never tell, but now, I don't know, maybe that was wrong.

A pang of loss shocked Tess with its intensity. Looking up from the letter, she found Detective Hill's gaze glued to her face. She said, "When...when did he die?"

"Ten weeks ago. December first."

"And you've read this letter?"

"It was in Katie's possession when she was hit outside her apartment building. One of her neighbors at the Vista Del Mar recognized her but didn't know her name and there was no ID in her wallet. The investigating officer found the letter. You can see that Katie wrote your phone number on the back. That's how we tracked you down."

Tess flipped the paper over and found her San Francisco phone number written in a different hand. "I see," she said woodenly.

He gestured at the paper and said, "Go on, finish reading it."

Turning the page over again, she read:

I know I told you your mother died in childbirth, but that's not the truth. Your mother didn't die. We split up when you were six months old. Only there's more.

You had a twin sister, identical to you. When everything fell apart, your mother and I decided we'd each take one of you. We actually rolled the dice to see which of you girls went where. You were so alike, there was just no other way to do it. I'm sorry for never telling you, but your mother and I made a pact and I'm breaking it now only because if I'm gone it means you're alone and I don't want that. I heard your mother went back to her maiden name of Mays after the divorce. Caroline Mays. Your sister's name is Theresa. I believe they resettled in California. Find them if you want, and if you do, well, tell your sister I'm sorry.

Forgive me, Katie.

Dad.

Ignoring the tears rolling down her cheeks, Tess refolded the letter. She looked up at Detective Hill, who regarded her with such empathy that it crumbled what little control she had left and she swayed on her feet again. Only, this time he caught her elbows in his strong hands and held her steady.

"There's more," he said in such a way that Tess understood at once that it wasn't good. He dropped his hands and shoved them in his pockets.

"Not yet," she murmured, wiping away the tears. "Give me a few moments." Directing her attention back to her sister, she added, "Is she…is she going to be okay?"

"The doctor said he thinks there's a good chance she'll pull through," he said. "Her brain waves are normal and her vital signs are decent. She hit her head hard when she went down, though—hence the concussion—but he said she could wake up tomorrow or next week. She's got bruises, torn ligaments in her right leg—I gather it's amazing her injuries aren't worse than they are."

"The person who called me said she'd been the victim of a hit-and-run. Has the driver come forward, have you found him yet?"

Detective Hill's eyes shifted uneasily as though he fervently wished he could respond with a positive, Of course! Instead he said, "There's not much to go on. There was one witness to the incident. A man walking his dog in the rain heard the impact and the squeal of brakes, but when he yelled, the driver, who had gotten out of the van, scrambled back inside and took off. Unfortunately, our witness is legally blind, but he can discern shapes and light. All he could say for certain was that the van was white. It didn't help that it was pouring cats and dogs. He couldn't tell if the driver was a man or a woman. There are a thousand white vans in New Harbor, Ms. Mays. Without a license plate…" His voice trailed off as he ran a hand through his black, glossy hair. "There's a whole lot you need to know."

Tess looked away from his gaze, staring at the bank of monitors, then at the face that was at once familiar and foreign—her twin sister. Her twin. All those years of loneliness and she'd had a twin the whole time.

And a father.

"Look, Ms. Mays—"

"Tess. Call me Tess."

"Okay. And please call me Ryan. You must be beat. Why don't I buy you a cup of coffee. This isn't the right place to talk."

"I need to call my mother. She needs to know about…Katie. She needs to…know."

The curtains parted as a middle-aged nurse swept into the room, nodding at Ryan as though used to seeing him there. Her glance at Tess was followed by a double take.

"I'm...I'm her sister," Tess said, trying the words on for size, flinching when she heard her voice utter them.

RYAN HILL STARED at the woman seated across from him. How could anyone look so much like someone else? And how could Matt Fields have kept a second daughter a secret all these years? *Wait a second... Theresa Mays was the least of Matt's secrets*.

The duplicate daughter was currently polishing off a stack of chocolate-chip pancakes topped with ice cream and doused with chocolate syrup. As she wiped up the last of the melted ice cream with the last bite of pancake, the waitress refilled their coffee cups.

Anxious to get out of the hospital, he'd hustled Tess to a diner down the block, thankful the relentless winter rain had stopped for a few moments. He hated that hospital. Peter had died there—technically, anyway. His real death had occurred in a flop house down near the tracks.

But that had been twelve years ago and until very recently, Ryan had managed to put his kid brother's miserable death and the part he himself had unwittingly played in that death behind him. This whole thing with Katie Fields had brought it back with a vengeance.

Tess finally put her fork down and, finding him looking at her, flashed him a guarded smile. "That was delicious."

He nodded, glancing at the wall clock. It was straight up on midnight. When it came to the middle of the night, he was a cup-of-black-coffee kind of guy.

"What do you do?" he asked. "I mean for a living?" He was trying to figure out how a petite woman like this one managed a stack of pancakes doused in ice cream. Maybe she dug ditches, though the pearly white of her skin suggested she worked indoors. Her clothes didn't look as if they belonged to a laborer, either. Tailored slacks fit her small but curvy figure perfectly, and the red blouse floating over her upper torso looked pricey. An executive of some type? If so, she was a far cry from her bartending, fun-loving sister.

"I'm a veterinarian," she said, brushing a few strands of hair away from her heart-shaped face. Her shoulder-length hair was wavy. He tried to recall what Katie's hair had looked like the last time he'd seen her but couldn't. To him, Katie had always been Matt's daughter, a nice enough woman he saw once or twice a year but never gave a second thought to when she was out of sight.

"Dogs and cats, mostly," she added, her smile deepening as she apparently thought of her patients.

"I have a cat," he said for no particular reason. Matt Fields's secret daughter was an animal doctor? Didn't a career choice like that take not only brains but conviction? Katie certainly was smart enough, but she always struck him as aimless. Because Tess looked like Katie, he'd expected her to be like Katie.

"You're staring at me," she said softly.

"Sorry."

She didn't respond but she looked unsettled and he didn't blame her. Less than twenty-four hours before, she'd been unique in the world, or so she'd thought. And now…

He said, "Did you reach your mother?"

She took a sip of coffee as the waitress reappeared to whisk away her plate. "No."

"She's not at home?"

"She just got married last weekend. One of

those whirlwind courtships. She and her new husband started out on their honeymoon to Seattle right after the ceremony, but I guess they haven't arrived yet. It's a long drive. I suppose they decided to take a side trip or two."

"It sounds as though you don't approve of your mother's spur-of-the-moment romance."

She blinked a couple of times and looked down at her hands. "My mother allowed one man to just about ruin her life. Now she expects another man to salvage it."

"And you don't believe in love at first sight."

She looked up at him, her eyes a summer blue, large in her small face. "No. Do you?"

He smiled. "No."

"You have to solve your own problems. You have to rely on yourself," she said. "Needing other people is tricky."

As a philosophy of life, it sounded lonely.

"Okay, let's get it over with," she said with a deep breath. "Tell me what's on your mind."

He folded his hands and adopted a serious expression, not hard to do since the topic was so grim. He said, "First, about your father—"

"Yes, my father," she said, her face lighting

up with an eagerness that touched him. "I want to know everything you can tell me about him. You said you were his partner. Tell me what he looked like, what he liked to do, start there, don't start with his death."

Matt Fields's death had been exactly where Ryan had intended to start. Reining in the impulse to blurt out the worst, he said, "Let's see. Your dad had graying brown hair and green eyes. About five-ten, 170 pounds. He was out of shape, didn't take care of himself, especially toward…well, the last. He wore glasses to read. I'm not sure about his hobbies. He was private. He liked his work…"

Ryan's voice trailed off. How well had he really known this woman's father? A couple of months ago he would have answered that with a laugh; hell, a cop gets to know his partner pretty damn well in four and a half years.

But he hadn't really known the guy at all. He knew that now. He suddenly recalled something he'd learned just recently. "Your dad liked to play the piano. He did it for charities, you know, in one of those little ensembles that perform at homes for the elderly or the disabled. Him and a couple of other guys. Nothing formal. It came out in the investigation afterward."

This seemed to please her. She smiled into her coffee cup.

"And, well, he adored your sister."

"But he never mentioned me?" she said, pinning him with that clear, blue gaze.

For a split second, Ryan thought of lying. He could make up a story and make her feel better and who would ever know? But he reached across the table and patted her hand. "I'm afraid not."

"I used to fantasize about him, you know?" she said. "Mom absolutely refused to talk about him, called him a cad, said she didn't even know his name, used him as a cautionary tale for premarital sex as I grew up. But I created stories about him anyway, larger-than-life-type fantasies. He was always searching for me in these daydreams, I was always just one day away from being found. And all the time, he knew more or less exactly where I was and didn't give a damn."

"I'm sorry—"

"No, please, don't be sorry." Looking him square in the eye, she said, "Tell me how he died."

At last. Ryan took a deep breath and met

her gaze. "A couple of months ago there was a fire. The woman trapped in the house was an invalid. Your dad—"

"The woman lived?"

"Yes. Your dad—"

"My father died a hero? This is what you've been wanting to tell me? That's wonderful. Oh, you know what I mean, not that he died, but that he died trying to save someone. Still, I imagine his unexpected death made Katie crazy."

He couldn't let her go on this way. He said, "No, Tess. Not a hero." For a second Ryan flashed back to that terrible night. By the time he'd arrived, the woman had been in the ambulance, her small dog yapping endlessly in a neighbor's arms. Matt was already dead; it was assumed he'd answered the fire call. That was before anyone realized he'd arrived before the call ever came.

"Ryan?"

"What I'm trying to tell you is that your dad shouldn't have been in that house. It was outside our district. He didn't know the family."

Tess looked puzzled. "Then how did he end up there?"

"Nobody knows for sure, but everyone

suspects. He sent me off on a wild-goose chase. By the time I found out about the fire, he was dead. What you need to understand is that the fire investigator found an accelerant on scene. That means arson."

He could tell she was beginning to sense the direction this talk was taking, and he hated himself for having to continue. He folded his hands together and pinned her with his gaze. "When a fire is purposely started, everybody involved gets investigated, and that includes the cops. Your dad died with huge gambling debts, Tess. I didn't even know he gambled, let alone on that scale. He'd lost almost everything he owned. Once the newspapers caught wind of his involvement, other stuff started surfacing. Kickbacks, extortions, bookies. I didn't know about any of it. I just thought he was a quiet guy. I didn't know he was addicted or crooked."

She stared at him with a deer-in-the-headlights gaze, tears blurring her lashes. "Are you sure?"

He nodded.

"You think my father started the fire?" She asked it as if she couldn't believe she'd heard him right. "Why would he do something like that?"

"Someone must have hired him."

"Who would hire a cop to burn down a house?"

"Someone who knew the cop was bent."

"Such as?"

"In this case, the logical suspect is the widow's stepson, a guy by the name of Nelson Lingford. A valuable art collection was mostly destroyed in the fire. Just a few paintings survived. If the insurance company can't link this back to Nelson, they will have to pay up, and the widow will collect a good chunk of change. Since she's relatively elderly, the money will go to Nelson."

"But why wouldn't he wait to inherit the collection itself?"

"Because it was about to be transferred to the museum to be assessed and catalogued. The widow was going to donate it—lock, stock and barrel. Once that had been completed, Nelson would have been out of luck. I don't imagine anyone was supposed to know the fire was arson."

"In other words, my father was supposed to make the fire look like an accident. So why not arrest this stepson?"

"There's nothing linking him to the fire or your father. Look, Madeline Lingford's late husband—Nelson's father—was a longtime businessman in New Harbor. After he died, Nelson took over, but he doesn't have his father's scruples. Some of his dealings have teetered on the edge of the law. Let's just say he's made his share of enemies. From what I hear, a former friend of Nelson's named Vince Desota lost his shirt on one of Nelson's deals. Since it's well known Nelson spent several evenings a week in residence at his stepmother's house, speculation has it old Vince decided to instigate a little payback."

"By destroying Nelson's stepmother's house?"

"And everything of value in the house, all of which would come to Nelson sooner or later, or so Vince probably thought. Like I said, it's speculation."

"So was Nelson Lingford at his stepmother's house that night?"

"Nope. Begged off at the last minute to attend a concert. Interesting, huh?" He stared at her a second before continuing. "Tess, your father's life was out of control. He apparently got caught in his own trap. They found receipts for a fuel can in his truck, the same kind found inside the house. They found a clerk down the coast who remembered him coming in and buying the damn thing. There was no fuel can at his apartment or in his truck or anywhere else except in that burned-out shell of a house. It was well known the widow was disabled and seldom left the place. A fire would kill her. Your dad would know that. I didn't want you hearing it from someone else."

"He tried to kill a woman?" Tess said, her eyes huge.

"I know it must come as a shock to you—"

"Oh, who cares about me? Poor Katie."

At that moment, for Ryan, Tess Mays stopped being a novelty, stopped being a carbon copy of her sister and turned into an individual. He searched his mind for a few comforting words to offer and came up short. He couldn't even reassure her about how Katie had taken it.

With a sigh he resolved to finish this. "That's not the worst of it," he mumbled at last, wishing the waitress would come back with the coffee and pour it over his head. He was suddenly freezing. Tess looked as though she was, too, and he fought an alarming desire to take her hands, to hold them close to his mouth and breath warm air on them.

"Tell me," she said, not meeting his eyes. "Just get it over with. My father—"

"It's not about your father," he said, interrupting. He took a deep breath. "It's about your sister."

"My God, what has *she* done?"

"It's not like that," he said quickly. He scanned the diner out of habit before lowering his voice and leaning over the table. "I don't think her 'accident' was an accident," he said with a knot in his throat. "I think someone purposely tried to run her down."

Tess gasped softly. "What are you saying?"

"I think someone tried to kill her."

Chapter Two

Tess ran her hands up and down her arms, aware for the first time that she wore a blouse so new there were probably tags still hanging down the back on the inside, attached to the label at the neck. She'd been in the process of dressing for work when the call from the Oregon police came. Dressing for work meant turtlenecks and lab coats. She didn't know how she'd come to choose the red silk; no doubt it just happened to be the first thing her fingers came in contact with.

And now it draped her body in soft, vulnerable, fragile wisps, and she wished she'd chosen something substantial, something strong...like body armor.

At any rate here she was twelve hours later sitting in a diner with a stranger, learning things about her family—a family she hadn't even known existed—that went from bad to startling and back again. The unmerciful overhead lights in the diner made the headache building behind her temples all the worse.

She got up abruptly, registering the startled look on Ryan Hill's face as she did so. "I'm·sorry," she murmured. He'd been talking, but his words had morphed into Swahili. She knew she couldn't sit still another moment. Digging in her shoulder bag—she'd left the duffel in her sister's hospital room—she produced a ten-dollar bill and slapped it on the table, then hurried through the restaurant and out the door, pulling on her coat as she walked, aware that he was following, embarrassed to be acting like a drama queen, but doing so, anyway.

The night air was cold and wet and fresh, salty with the nearby sea, invigorating, just what she needed. She pulled her lightweight coat close about her body, shivering despite herself, head tilted down against the rain. It might be wetter than usual in San Francisco this year, but it wasn't cold like this, the wind didn't bite at you, the raindrops didn't ricochet off the sidewalk and nip your skin.

Ryan Hill's long-legged stride being twice hers, she'd known he'd catch up with her quickly if he wanted to. He didn't grab her arm, for which she was grateful, just hunkered down and slowed his gait to match hers, staying right by her side. His presence was reassuring.

Eventually they reached the corner, and she had a decision to make. To the left lay the hospital and her sister, lost in a coma, unaware Tess had come to see if her existence could possibly be true. To the right lay the ocean, albeit some way off. She turned right, which meant she was walking more or less into the wind. Her hair whipped around her face and plastered her damp clothes against the front of her trembling body.

"You're going to freeze to death," Ryan finally said. "Hell, I'm going to freeze to death."

"I know," she said. And then after a few more steps, head still down, added, "Go on, talk."

"Let me know if you can't make sense of what I'm saying through my chattering teeth," he said.

She smiled down at the glistening sidewalk. "Okay."

"I was talking about your sister. How much did you hear me say?"

"Not much."

"Then I'll start over, but this time you're getting the abbreviated version for obvious reasons." He paused, she guessed to organize his thoughts, then proceeded. "Katie came to see me after Matt died. She thought the department was making him a scapegoat or maybe that he'd been framed. She was in complete denial, unwilling or unable to see the facts. Her dad couldn't have done something so awful. He just wouldn't. She was adamant."

Tess's lips twisted into a wry smile as her sister took on dimensions as a human being, evolving from an injured figure to a real live woman. She liked knowing this about Katie—that she was loyal and true. "Go on," Tess said.

"I refused to help her," Ryan said, his voice ragged. "I refused. My career was on the line. I was Matt's partner and Matt was crooked, ergo, I was suspect, an internal investigation was probing into both of us. I think Matt sent me off chasing phantoms that night not only to get me out of the way but to make sure I had an alibi. Anyway, the department told me to stay far away from this case. The Lingfords are a prominent family in the community despite the rumors of shady dealings, and the D.A. is unwilling to point a finger in their direction until there's proof. Vince Desota hasn't made a single move to indicate guilt, but sooner or later—*if* he's guilty—he's bound to let something slip to someone, and the detective on this case has his ear close to the ground. Plus there are other people connected with the family. Or it could have been an attempted art heist, the fire a diversion that went awry. I told Katie to be patient and trust the system."

He stopped talking as he touched her elbow and guided her around another corner. The wind hit with renewed ferocity, blowing open Tess's coat, biting through the silk blouse. A hotel lobby opening to the street lay a few steps ahead. Ryan pushed open the door. She paused only a second before sidling past him.

The steamy heat of the lobby hit her with a bang. She stopped and took a deep breath.

"There's a bar over in the corner," he said, taking her elbow and steering her toward the lounge as he spoke. "We'll get something hot to drink."

He chose a small, round table and as she took off her wet coat, longing for a towel to pat dry her hair, he went to the bar and came back with two stemmed glass mugs of Irish coffee, the cream floating on top like melted clouds.

They both wrapped their hands around the hot glasses and breathed in the fragrant brew.

"What happened next?" she asked.

He picked up the conversation as though it hadn't been interrupted for several minutes and said, "Your sister said she understood."

"Just like that?" The thought flashed across Tess's mind that Katie wouldn't have given up that easily. Tess knew *she* wouldn't have.

"Just like that. I was relieved. But when I tried to call her the next week, her number had been disconnected and there was no new listing. I went by her place and found that she'd moved out the week before. Ditto at the latest place she told me she'd been working, a lounge out at the city limits."

"A lounge?"

"She tends bar. Hell, she does lots of different things. Your dad said she couldn't make up her mind what she wanted."

Tess sat there and tried to absorb this. She'd spent her entire life knowing exactly what she wanted to do. The idea that someone who looked just like her could be so different was startling.

"Anyway, they said she left their employ the same day she left her apartment. Still, there didn't seem to be any cause for alarm. She'd just lost her dad in a terrible way, so I figured she needed to go off by herself for a while."

Tess took a sip of whiskey-laced coffee, licked the cream off her upper lip and wrapped her hands back around the glass mug. The alcohol spread through her body, melting icy niches with heady warmth. "I don't understand why you think you're to blame for her accident. I mean, obviously she went away to think and then came back to New Harbor—"

"I should have known she gave in too easy. Katie was passionate about your father's innocence."

"Ryan, I'm still not understanding—"

"The investigating traffic officer didn't like the scene of Katie's accident. For one thing, there were no skid marks, for another the driver went up on the curb but missed a telephone pole he or she should have hit. Then there's the fact that the driver got out of the van and didn't run away until the dog walker yelled."

Tess closed her eyes for a moment. The whiskey had moved to her head. She tried to imagine her sister walking down the sidewalk as a white van barreled toward her. Katie wouldn't have just stood there waiting to be hit. She must have been distracted. Had she realized what was coming in the split second before metal hit skin and bone?

"I told you they checked her purse and found the letter your father left her but no identification. The traffic officer recognized Matt's name on the letter. It took a few hours for someone to get ahold of me. By that time Katie was as you see her now, comatose, unreachable."

Tess still wasn't sure what Ryan was saying. Her expression must have betrayed her confusion because without waiting for her to think of the right question to ask, he added, "I think she'd been poking around. My guess is she came across something someone was hiding."

"And so they tried to kill her?"

"Exactly. If I hadn't fallen for the way she

blew me off that day, if I hadn't been worried about my own future and been so angry with Matt for betraying me and everything I thought he stood for, I might have been able to talk some real sense into her. I might have been able to prevent this."

Tess stared hard at him. There was genuine pain in his eyes—pain and guilt. And it seemed out of proportion to his story. Did a man in his line of work take responsibility for everyone they knew, every problem that crossed their path?

"But at least you know where to start, right?" she said slowly. "I mean, it must be that stepson. Or that Desota guy. You find which of them has a white van and you arrest them and then they tell us what happened to Katie's father—" She caught herself and amended, "To our father. This could be a big break, right?"

"I've already done all that. There's no white van registered to Nelson Lingford. No rentals, either. As for Vince Desota? He owns a few vans—he runs an electrical contractor business, and yes, they're white. None unaccounted for or damaged. It'll take time to go through Nelson's other enemies, and unless there's an official investigation, it won't do much good anyway. There's no proof that Katie's hit-and-run wasn't an accident. The traffic officer signed it off. It's been lousy weather and there have been a lot of traffic accidents lately."

Tess stared at her empty mug. "I see. I think."

"And there's one last thing," Ryan added. "The last number dialed on her cell phone was mine. I wasn't in the office and she didn't leave a message. I guess she didn't have my cell phone number, just the department's. The time recorded for the call is compatible with our witness's estimation of when the accident occurred. She was walking to or from her car, we think, when she was hit. I can't help wondering if she was coming to find me."

"So she tried to reach you."

"Yes." He took a swallow of his coffee and added, "What I'm trying to say is simple. I'm sorry."

She met his gaze and nodded.

He put a few bills on the table as he stood up. "You must be dead on your feet. Did you get a hotel already? If not, there's nothing wrong with this place. I'll go get your bag and—"

"I don't want a hotel," she said. "I'll spend the night in Katie's room."

"That's not a good idea."

She stood, too, still forced to look up at him because of their height difference. "This isn't your decision to make, Detective Hill."

He appeared startled by her comment, as though he wasn't used to being crossed. He appeared to be a solid, healthy man used to taking control, caring but persistent, the kind who expected to shoulder every burden. There was another element to him, as well, that lurking hurt she'd seen behind his eyes.

"I can't offer you forgiveness for how you reacted or didn't react when Katie asked for help," she said, choosing her words carefully. "I'm not my sister, I can't absolve you for her."

"I know," he said softly.

"Then—"

"I'm not asking for you to forgive me," he said, his gray eyes smoldering. "I know I screwed up. I know I let her down. I thought of myself...I should have—"

He stopped himself, shook his head and added, "I'm just trying to explain why I'm back in the game. If I can't find out what happened to Katie from within the department, then I'll take vacation time and figure it out on my own. It's as easy as that."

She had no idea what to make of this guy. She'd never met anyone quite like him.

He added, "I'm also going to make sure you stay in one piece, Ms. Mays."

Annoyed, she snapped, "I'm not your concern."

"Hasn't it occurred to you that whatever happened to Katie could happen to you?"

"Why should it? *I'm* not a threat."

"No, *you* aren't a threat. You just happen to look like the woman someone might have found so threatening they tried to kill her."

Tess shuddered deep inside. She was a veterinarian, not a policewoman, not an adventurer, not brave or resolute or any of the rest. She'd grown up sheltered from violence, quietly accepting her role as her troubled mother's keeper, turning to animals for comfort and companionship. She didn't even know her sister, couldn't remember one single thing about her father. For this she might be risking her neck?

Her life back in San Francisco—the clinic, the animals, her partners, her friends—suddenly seemed a zillion miles away.

Where in the hell was her mother? The woman had some major explaining to do.

"At least let me walk you back to the hospital," Ryan said.

She nodded, not meeting his gaze, half ashamed of her gutlessness.

And half terrified.

RYAN SPENT THE NIGHT trapped in a restless dream where he tried to find his kid brother, running down one empty street after another. Every time he seemed to get close, however, Peter's frightened voice would fade away and begin again somewhere else and Ryan would be off again.

He'd had the same dream a hundred times and it never got any easier. He never found Peter, and he was unable to save him. It was a relief to wake up to no one but his cat.

"Morning, Clive," he said. Clive, as usual, sat perched on the foot of Ryan's bed, wearing his inscrutable cat gaze. A trim black wraith, he lived in a secret world of his own Ryan only occasionally caught a glimpse of. Clive had taken the concept of the mysterious cat to heart.

Ryan's next thought was of Tess, of the last he'd seen of her, sitting in the stiff little chair beside her sister's bed, yawning into her hand, looking small and alone. She might act tough, but he suspected it was a front. He'd wanted to take her to his house and protect her from he didn't know what, but he'd made himself walk away.

And now he knew what he had to do next. First he'd go into work and read every file he could get his hands on, get caught up on Matt's case, settle a few loose ends with Jason Hyatt, his new partner, then put in for three weeks of accumulated vacation. In that time he would make sure Tess Mays got home safely and stayed there, then he'd find out what happened to Katie and maybe even what happened to Matt. Clear the whole thing up, move on.

Simple. He should have done it before. Clive meowed, a throaty, strangled sound that meant it was time for breakfast.

"I suppose that's your way of ordering eggs Benedict," he told the cat who blinked yellow eyes.

AS THE DAY WORE ON the huge hospital became increasingly small to Tess. The high point was meeting with Katie's doctor and being told indications suggested a good chance of a full recovery, but he refused to be narrowed down to particulars. "Maybe today, maybe tomorrow, maybe next month," was all the doctor would commit himself to.

After that, she'd tried yet again to reach her mother's new husband's son—her new step-brother, she realized with a start—a thirty-seven-year-old man named Nick Pierce who lived in some remote Alaskan town. Despite her mother's efforts to get him down to California for his father's wedding, he hadn't come and the housekeeper who answered the phone this time would only say he was un-available.

The wedding, the honeymoon, a new life…it was all surreal to Tess. Up to this point, her mother's idea of adventure had been ordering Chinese food. She'd spent most of Tess's life hiding from reality, doing nothing but working, sleeping and reading, almost in equal proportions, frozen in twen-ty-seven years of grief Tess had never under-stood.

Until now. Her mother had lived a hideous lie. She'd divided her children and been party to hiding the truth, something that ob-viously ate at her until Mr. Seattle swept into her life and somehow, finally, provided a distraction. If Tess was to be honest, she'd been weak with relief that someone else had come along to shoulder some of her mother's care, meet some of her mother's insatiable need.

But it was all pretend, a fantasy her mother created to fill a void. If her mother's lesson had been to distrust a woman's need of a man, Tess had learned it well. Too bad her mother hadn't followed her own counsel.

After a short shower and a welcome change of clothes in a facility the nurse pointed out, Tess walked endless hallways that all looked the same, read countless magazines and called work where she was told to take all the time she needed, family comes first.

Family.

The word had a whole new concept.

Several times she stood by the window at the end of the hall and looked out at the rain-swept city, wishing she was brave enough to go out the front door. But she stayed inside, not only because Ryan Hill had warned her to but because, face it, she was a chicken and she didn't want someone pointing a great big white van at her.

But honestly, was a van a very clever murder weapon? Wouldn't a knife or an assault rifle get the job done better? After all, her sister wasn't dead, she was injured and expected to recover.

By late afternoon Tess had found the scrap of paper on which she'd written Ryan's phone number. She stared at it. Tempted to call him, she left Katie's room before she crumbled. She knew why she wanted to hear his voice—she wanted reassurance. The thought that she might be turning into a woman as weak and needy as her mother wasn't a pleasant one. A few minutes later she caught a cab outside the hospital.

It took barely ten minutes for the taxi to roll to a stop in front of Vista Del Mar Apartments. Tess paid the driver and stood on the sidewalk, glad the rain had let up, wishing the wind would take a hint and follow suit.

Perhaps at one time a view of the ocean had been a possibility from the windows of the Vista Del Mar, but development around the old structure made that something of the past. The building itself was two stories of gray cement, dwarfed by the high-rise condos on either side. It looked like a poor relation, hovering in the shadows, apologetic and self-conscious.

Tess stared up and down the darkening street. Across from a large park, numerous

driveways led to high-rise condos. The telephone pole Ryan had mentioned the driver
of the white van missing had to be one of a
string running along the park side and one of
the cars parked along the sidewalk might
well belong to Katie.

Tess closed her eyes for a second, pictur-
ing Katie walking fast, head bent down
against the rain. Her sister would have looked
up when she heard an approaching engine. A
blur of white metal, the shock of impact—

Tess opened her eyes, her heart racing.

What was she doing here?

Fear had held her hostage in the hospital
until boredom made fear look downright
agreeable by comparison. Tess was a take-
charge woman in her own life. She'd studied
hard, secured a good job right out of college,
worked even harder once employed. She
hadn't had this much idle time since…well,
since she couldn't remember when.

At any rate, she'd felt the need to come to
this place. Now she was here and, despite the
bravado that had provided the impetuous,
she kind of wished she weren't.

She reached into her purse and found her
cell phone, trying once again to make it
work, but she still had no coverage this far

north. How was she supposed to call a cab, and even if she could, where was she supposed to go?

Back to the hospital? No, thanks.

You could go to Katie's apartment, a voice sounded inside her head. *You could stand at her door and touch the knob she last touched and maybe, maybe...*

Maybe what?

Tess, rubbed her temples.

"Well, hello there!" cried a woman being pulled through the door by an anxious Dalmatian on a lead.

Startled, Tess said, "I beg your pardon?"

The woman struggled with the dog. "I'm just surprised to see you back here. From what Frances said, I thought you'd be in the hospital for days. Hey, what did you do to your hair?"

"My hair?" Tess said, her hand automatically touching her blond, windblown tresses.

But the woman, now halfway across the street thanks to the apparently desperate dog, only waved her free hand.

Before the door swung shut again, Tess slipped into the foyer. Relieved to get out of the wind, she paused to scan the row of mailboxes. Two or three slots were labeled with

name tags, the others weren't. She stood
there for a moment, looking down the short
hall on the first floor. With a shake of her
head, she made an arbitrary decision: Katie
would not live on the ground floor.

She took a ratty elevator to the second
floor where she found an older man
fumbling with his keys while struggling with
two grocery bags. One of the paper sacks
looked as though the bottom was about to
fall out of it. "Need help?" she asked hoping
to earn directions to her sister's apartment
for her trouble.

The old man looked at her over his
shoulder, a scowl making his wrinkled face
resemble an apple carving, rheumy eyes
awash with hostility. "No!" he snarled.
"Leave me be."

"Sorry," she said, backing away. His anger
was almost palpable but she doubted it was
truly directed at her—or Katie. The man
appeared mad at the world. He finally got his
door open and went inside, using his foot to
slam it behind him.

"All righty, then..." she mumbled.

There were five additional doors leading
off the hall. Tess began knocking on each
one. She'd ask the first person to answer to

point her in the right direction. The only problem with her plan was that no one seemed to be home. She found an apartment across the hall and down one with a Dalmatian doorknocker—easy to imagine who lived here! Maybe she should go outside and wait for the woman with the dog to come back and point the way.

Knocking on the last door at the end of the hall, she was surprised when it flew inward at the first touch. "Hello?" she called. "Anyone home?"

The apartment was dark, but light from the hall illuminated a wedge of wall at right angles to the door. In that wedge of light hung a framed photograph that caught Tess's attention immediately, and she stared at it with wonder. The photo was of a six-year-old child sitting in a wading pool and a man standing alongside, the two connected by a glistening stream of water arcing between his hose and the child's pool.

Tess's heart stopped beating. The child could have been her, except that Tess had never had a wading pool. And the man? Her father, undoubtedly, and she'd never had one of those, either. She touched the image of his face with her fingertip, trying to see something of herself in his features. This was Katie's apartment. This was a picture of their father.

For a second Tess thought of the times ahead, God willing. The getting-to-know-you phase where she and Katie would review their childhoods, the informational phase where they'd each learn about the parent they didn't know from the sister they didn't know and, eventually, the build-a-future phase where they would finally get to be twins, finally get to share their lives. How *odd* that would be. How odd and how wonderful....

Tess flipped on the light. She gasped. Drawers had been pulled out and emptied; cabinets flung open, contents spilled onto the carpet; cushions slashed and thrown aside; knickknacks broken against the wall as if in spite.

Fear came back with a body slam. What in the world was she doing in a place that had recently, she assumed, known such violence? Ryan's words of warning suddenly seemed perceptive rather than paranoid. She stepped back into the hallway, her hand on the knob.

And paused.

If she left right now, she'd lose whatever modicum of control she had by virtue of apparently being the first person on scene. Alone she could search the rubble for more photos. She could get a sense of Katie's life. And that's why she'd come, that's why she'd been drawn here. If she left, she might never be welcomed back.

She stepped inside and waited a second. The place had the feel of emptiness. Whatever had happened here was over.

Decision made, she closed the door behind her, noticing for the first time that the door frame was splintered where the lock had been broken. Stifling a renewed trickle of alarm, she made her way to a pile of books in front of built-in shelves. Maybe in that jumble she'd find a photo album. She'd search fast and get out.

She'd barely begun digging through the chaos when she heard a noise in the hall like approaching footsteps. In a blink, without thinking, she stumbled over the debris and hit the light switch, plunging the room back into darkness. She expected to hear voices, keys, a dog, the sounds of a close-by apartment door opening and shutting. But though she strained to hear a nice, ordinary, unscary sound that signaled someone benign, she heard…nothing.

She backed deeper into the room, stepping over glass and shattered pottery, overturned plants and clothing, her own noises in the dark sounding more like an elephant stampede than a furtive retreat. A tingling in her scalp let her know that for some reason she was afraid.

The sound in the hall stopped. Tess stood absolutely still for what seemed a century.

Finally she took a deep breath. Nerves had gotten the best of her. Spying definitely wasn't in her future.

The steps started again, closer this time. They sounded stealthy. Surely another door would open and close as a neighbor came home.

The footsteps stopped outside Katie's door.

Heart racing, Tess hugged the wall and backed into the bedroom, feeling her way, grateful there were few wall ornaments on which to bump her head. Stumbling over rubble, she found the bedroom closet, slipped inside and tugged the door. It was stuck open. She flattened herself between hanging clothes and the wall.

Footfalls came from inside the apartment. A tinkle of glass. A muffled oath. Her heart beat like a jungle drum, crashed against her ribs like a bumper car.

The bedroom light came on suddenly, the clothes in front of her jerked aside. Tess threw up an arm to cover her eyes.

A hand closed on her wrist and pulled it down.

She found herself staring into the barrel of a gun.

Chapter Three

"Tess, it's okay, it's me," Ryan Hill said.

She threw herself against Ryan's chest, melted against him in a heap, cried despite the relief or maybe because of it. He held her and soothed her, the gun still in his right hand, his left patting her back.

"You scared me!" she finally said, pushing herself away.

"I know. I'm sorry," he said. "Are you okay? Were you here when the place was turned upside down? Did anyone hurt you?"

He pulled her toward him as he said these things, and she shook her head, tears rolling down her cheeks, glad when her head hit his chest again.

His leather jacket was cool and smooth against her cheek, but the man beneath was rock hard and warm. In the moment he'd looked at her, she'd seen his gray eyes flood with concern, his stern expression soften. His breath ruffled her hair, whispered by her forehead, and she closed her eyes. She said, "I wasn't here. I came afterward."

"Let me get this straight," he said with an edge to his voice. "You came into this apartment knowing it had been ransacked?"

Her eyes popped open. She didn't like that edge, probably, she admitted to herself, because she'd more or less earned it. Still, this man wasn't her keeper, and the out-of-place attraction she'd been fighting a moment before fled in a wave of irritation as she shrugged herself free from his one-handed grip.

As she searched the room for something on which to dry her tears, she said, "I knew the intruder was gone." It amazed her that her voice sounded so strong. By all rights, it should be as shaky as her knees.

"How did you know?"

"It *felt* empty," she said, spying a tissue box next to the overturned mattress. She climbed over the tangled knot of a pink quilt and snagged the box. Mopping at her face, she looked around the trashed room.

He shook his head as he slipped his gun

back into the shoulder holster he wore under his jacket. "It *felt* empty?"

"Let it go," she said, eyes flashing.

He stared at her.

"What are *you* doing here?" she demanded.

"You weren't at the hospital when I called. I asked myself where I'd go if I were you, and this is what I came up with."

"And scared me nearly to death!" she repeated, but it wasn't the fear that rankled, it was the humiliation of having broken down in front of him. She was willing to do almost anything now to distance herself from that clinging vine, that needy, weepy thing she'd become in the aftermath of intense fear. Anything was better than that.

"Well, no harm done," she said briskly.

"That's right," he said, a wicked gleam igniting his eyes, "no harm done. Except that I might have been the bad guy back for a second look."

Tess stared at her feet. She knew he was right, but she wasn't going to let him see that. He'd already seen too much. She said, "I'm going to clean up this place. I don't want Katie coming home to something like this. Maybe I'll figure out what's missing."

He regarded her with raised eyebrows.

"How in the world will you know what's missing in an apartment you've never been in before?"

"I haven't the slightest idea," she answered. *But she would know*. She just wasn't going to try to explain something to him she couldn't explain to herself. It was like knowing Katie wouldn't so easily quit trying to figure out who framed their father or that she lived on the second floor of this building. *She just knew*.

"Well it's immaterial, anyway," he said, taking out his cell phone. "You can't do anything in here until the scene is processed. So find someplace to sit down, and try not to touch anything else, okay?"

She glared at him.

"Please," he added.

Of course it had to be processed. "I'll go sit on what's left of the big recliner," she said.

He nodded as he spoke into the phone.

RYAN ASKED EVERYONE who answered their door if they'd seen anyone or anything suspicious in the past thirty-six hours, since Katie Fields had been hit by that white van.

No one had ever heard of Katie Fields.

No one there knew the name of the tenant in 206. The manager would know, but he was off in Hawaii.

The woman with the dog confessed she played music almost continually to cover the noise of her almost-deaf neighbor's television. She did mention Frances from downstairs, who knew everybody and everything but who worked nights. The old grouch across from the elevator said, "I ain't a snoop like some people."

One person wasn't home, and the last one, the elderly lady with a hearing problem, admitted she had no idea who lived, "down at that end of the hall."

That was the trouble. Katie's apartment was the last one on the left. The unit across from hers was empty, the lady with the dog told him, and had been for weeks. The unit under hers belonged to the vacationing manager.

Ryan's partner and a couple of guys from the lab were finishing looking through Katie's apartment, but it was such a low priority that it was more or less being done because Ryan had asked. He didn't expect the person who'd done this to have left fingerprints or telltale hairs.

Which, he decided as he leaned against the

wall in the hall, was just as well. He didn't want to get warned away from looking into Katie Fields's mishap. He wanted it to remain a hit-and-run and not get bumped up to attempted murder or linked to her father's death.

Jason came out and lit a cigarette, something he did more or less every ten minutes when possible. He was younger than Ryan by a year or two, chatty and full of himself, as different from Matt Fields as night is from day.

"I can't believe old Matt had himself another daughter," Jason said, expelling a cloud of foul smoke.

Ryan waved his hand in front of his face. "They probably have rules about smoking in this place," he said. "Well, as we both know, Matt was full of secrets. You guys find anything?"

"In that mess? Looks like there are two sets of prints. One all over the place, probably the victim's, the other set belongs to the victim's sister. You know how it is, people see an ambulance take away a victim and the next thing you know, some creep goes in and robs her blind, and everyone knows to wear gloves now. I don't see a computer or TV or anything so maybe they took off with that kind of stuff. Ditto on jewelry. You ask the neighbors if anyone saw anything or if any of them are familiar with Katie's apartment and can tell if something is missing?"

"No one on this floor saw anything and no one had ever been invited inside, though one woman said she believed the apartment was rented furnished." He gave Jason the name and workplace for Frances from downstairs. "You check her out. I'll give it an hour or so for people to settle in for the night and try the rest of the ground floor, but I imagine it'll be the same."

CSI came out of the apartment next. They shot the breeze for a few minutes, then left and Ryan stayed where he was, in the hall, thinking about going back inside.

He kind of regretted getting so uppity with Tess, but she'd scared him to death, then touched his heart with her trembling and tears, then had turned into a smart aleck. He'd put her in her place because he needed to put *himself* in *his* place. He was determined to protect his late partner's daughters whether they liked it or not, and he couldn't afford to let this pretty veterinarian with the bluest eyes this side of Tahiti get in his way.

Damn it, but he had to admit he'd enjoyed her moment of need. He'd liked her holding on to him like he was a lifeline. She'd felt good in his arms. A natural fit. Talk about screwy, but he'd been disappointed when she turned back into herself. And he knew this was crazy, counterproductive and downright dangerous for both her safety and his peace of mind, so he had to get ahold of himself and the situation and he thought he knew how to do it.

Pep talk delivered, he pushed open the door and went back inside.

She was down on her knees, stuffing pillow innards into a garbage bag. He rested on his haunches and held the bag for her so she could use both hands.

"I'm sorry about all this," he said.

She glanced up at him. "Thanks."

"Tess, don't bite my head off, but I think you ought to go home tomorrow."

She went back to work, moving from cushion stuffing to broken pieces of pottery too small to put back together again. At last she said, "I don't think Katie intended on staying here long."

Obviously, she had chosen to ignore his suggestion. No matter, he would approach it again from a different angle. She wasn't a fool, and she didn't strike him as impetuous like her sister, but there was a hint of stubbornness reminiscent of Katie that might make getting rid of her tricky. He said, "What makes you think that?"

"Your partner pointed out the lack of electronic equipment as though it might have been stolen, but I don't think she had any. There's no desk for a computer, there are no CDs lying around or tapes or cords or anything else. There's no telephone jack. It's still hard to tell, but I think Katie either traveled light or she stored most of her belongings somewhere and moved in here with just a few sentimental frills."

"I think you might be right. She wasn't using her real name here, that's obvious. She wasn't making friends and visiting with the neighbors which strikes me as out of character for her. She was up to something."

"How about my father's house?"

"What do you mean?"

"Well, I assume Katie no longer lived with him, but maybe she left most of her stuff at his place. He must have had a house—"

"He did. A nice one, but it was repossessed by the bank for nonpayment. It was part of that noose-closing-in-on-him thing. Matt was living out of a suitcase at the end."

She looked pale. "I see."

Ryan wished he'd picked up just a little of his late partner's secret-keeping abilities. "I know how to do my job," he said. "You go home. I'll keep you posted on Katie's condition, and I promise you I'll keep at this until the bitter end."

He took the plastic bag from her as they both stood. For a second they stared at each other. Out of the corner of his eye, Ryan caught a glimpse of their reflections in the window. He seemed to loom over her and yet she held her own, a slip of a woman dressed now in jeans and a sweater, her fair hair askew, her posture perfect. He had a sudden recollection of the feel of her body slammed tight against his chest.

Tossing the bag aside, he made his way to the wall and closed the drapes against the night.

"You can't stay here," he said, turning back to her.

"Don't start with me," she warned, picking up a handful of paperbacks.

"The lock is broken. Whoever did this might come back."

He saw a flash of terror cross her face. He'd put that terror there. Shame on him.

"I have to stay," she said at last. "I have to look through Katie's things. If I'm going to go home in a day or so—"

"So you agree to leave?" he asked hopefully, and yet with a peculiar sense of loss.

"Yes, okay, I'll go home. I know I'm not cut out to chase bad guys. Maybe I can get Katie transferred to a hospital closer to me or I can fly up here on the weekends—anyway, that's why this may be my last chance…"

Her voice trailed off.

Her last chance to get to know Katie in case she didn't recover from her injuries? Her last chance to get a feeling for a father who might very well have aspired to be a cold-blooded murderer? Her last chance to find missing pieces of herself?

He'd gone and frightened her again. His feelings were raw and banging into each other, making him say and do things in an awkward, stilted manner. Still, no matter how disjointed his words and actions, his motive was pure—he would not let anything happen to Tess Mays, he would not let her down.

"If you stay here tonight, I stay," he said, expecting an argument.

But she didn't argue, in fact there was relief in her eyes and in her voice. "Okay."

"And tomorrow morning, you make arrangements to go back to San Francisco where you belong."

She nodded. "By then maybe we'll have figured out how Katie went about her snooping."

"That's right," he said, glancing at the mess in which they stood. "We have our work cut out for us."

With that, he reached for his cell phone. He needed to get his neighbor to feed Clive. He needed to order takeout. He needed to do something, anything, other than look at Tess Mays and entertain thoughts that would get him absolutely nowhere.

RYAN EMPTIED THE CONTENTS of the brown envelope he'd brought from the police evidence room onto the table between them. He'd eaten most of his hamburger and fries and half drunk the chocolate shake. He'd also talked to Jason. Frances from downstairs had slept the afternoon away. She hadn't seen or heard anything unusual.

The food choice had been Tess's idea. Ryan had argued for Thai, but she announced she'd had a miserable day and that called for fast food.

"Hand me an apple pie," she said.

He handed her the white paper sack and watched as she retrieved a warm pastry. "How do you stay so slim when you eat this kind of stuff?" he asked.

She licked a glob of gooey apple from her lips. The action caused a wave of desire in his groin that hit him hard and unexpected.

"I run. I work out," she said. "Believe it or not, on a day-to-day basis, I'm not usually stressed like this so I don't always eat like this."

"Allow me to clean up," he said, standing quickly to bag their rubble, relieved to move away from the table—away from her.

THE ENVELOPE CONTAINED a still ticking gold watch, a turquoise ring and earrings, a very small red purse on a very long cord Katie must have looped around her neck and shoulder containing no identification of any kind. The wallet was there, just no identification as though she didn't carry any. She had thirteen dollars and twenty seven cents, and a short list of phone numbers with no names. There was also a cell phone, a pair of shattered glasses with black frames and a ring with five keys and a dolphin fob. One key got Katie in the Vista's lobby door, Ryan explained, as it had also gotten him in. One opened her mail box, one opened her apartment, one started her car and the last one was unexplained though it was stamped with the number 119.

"What about the glasses?"

"I don't know," he said. "There's no correction in the lenses, there's some question they're even hers. I know I never saw her wear glasses. The officer on scene found them in the gutter and picked them up, but they might have been there for hours for all we know."

Tess flipped the phone open. The battery was low when she turned it on, but she flipped through the options until she could access the photo gallery.

And sure enough, in among the photos of strangers, there was a picture of Katie and the same man—only twenty years older—as in the picture on the wall. It looked as if it was taken at a park during the summer.

"The police picnic," Ryan said, peering over her shoulder. "Katie asked me to take this. They'd just won the ubiquitous three-legged race."

Tess drank in the sight of the two smiling faces, one identical to her own, the other lost forever, and felt a knot form in her throat. "Have you checked the phone records?" she managed to say at last.

"As in, Did she call her would-be attacker or snap a picture of a speeding white van?"

"Something like that."

"No such luck. Very few calls, none unexplained except that last one made to me. As far as I can tell, the last picture is this one." He clicked a few buttons and up came a tiny photo of a trophy.

"Whose trophy?"

"Your guess is as good as mine. I can't make out any writing. Too much glare."

Tess scrolled up a picture, hoping for something more meaningful and found a shot of a very young woman who looked slightly off-kilter. Maybe it was her eyes, Tess thought, looking closely. She appeared to be mentally handicapped. That was it. But she looked happy and friendly, and she was wearing a pointy pink party hat.

"Who's this?"

"I don't know. Obviously someone Katie knew."

Tess nodded absently as she clicked back to the photo of her sister and father, once again drinking in their smiles before the battery gave up the ghost and their images faded away.

FOR TESS THE JOB at hand was bittersweet.

The objects of Katie's life lay shattered and torn in her apartment, the same way her body lay battered in the hospital. But there was a sense of the woman here, reflected in little things like the umpteen tiny packets of mustard, ketchup and taco sauce that filled a box in the fridge—they apparently shared the same love of junk food—the simple white dress hanging in the closet, the secondhand paperback mystery books.

To her regret there were no additional photos. Not a baby picture, not a strip of goofy poses from the mall…nothing. There was no rent receipt with a name, no bank statement, no pay stub or tax forms. Katie had lived in New Harbor her whole life and yet Tess couldn't find an address book or a note from a friend or the name of a dentist circled in the phone book. Nothing. The conviction that Katie had chosen this apartment from which to launch her investigation grew as the hours passed.

The living room was soon back to as normal as it was going to get without a few purchases to replace the things that had been destroyed. Tess sat down in front of the bedroom closet and started putting the half-dozen pairs of shoes and the half-dozen empty shoe boxes back together.

The moment she dumped a pair of leather boots—her exact size and even a style she would have chosen—into their box, she realized something else was stuffed beneath the layer of tissue paper on the bottom. She lifted the tissue, which had been taped onto a false bottom, then immediately looked over her shoulder to see if Ryan had come into the room. The coast was clear, but she closed the box, anyway. She'd caught a glimpse of what was hidden inside. Just a glimpse, but the objects looked personal and she wanted to study them without Ryan hovering nearby.

Going back into the living room, she found he'd fallen asleep on the recliner. A few pages of sheet music lay scattered across his lap and spilled onto the floor as though he'd been looking at them when he drifted off. Tess approached quietly, gathered the papers without his waking, then stood staring down at him.

Dark lashes fanned his cheeks. His mouth in repose looked soft and sensual. His head rested on one hand bent at the elbow and propped against the back of the chair, his long jeans-clad legs were crossed at the ankles.

Her gut reaction to the sight of him sleeping stunned her with its intensity. She tried to drag her gaze away but she couldn't. She'd never reacted like this to a near stranger, and it annoyed her at the same time fascinating her. Her heart fluttered. Her fingertips tingled with the desire to trace the line of his jaw and maybe kiss his throat, where she could see the healthy throb of his pulse.

She bet he'd had his share of love affairs.

Had he had one with Katie?

It didn't seem likely. But if he didn't find Katie attractive, how could he find *her* attractive?

Get a grip on yourself, she mumbled, and resisted the urge to smooth a lock of dark hair away from his eyes, knowing it was nothing more than an excuse to touch him and to start something she couldn't, wouldn't, finish. She turned to tiptoe back to the bedroom and the shoebox.

But first she examined the sheet music.

She, too, played piano. A smile lifted the corners of her lips as she noted she played some of these very pieces. There were many faded handwritten notes on the pages and even a scribbled date or two going back ten or more years.

My father's music. She bit her lip as tears stung behind her nose.

Setting it aside, she sank to her knees and opened the shoe box again, carefully lifting out the false bottom.

The first item she encountered was a small bound notebook. She flipped it open, heart in her throat, thinking perhaps she had just come across a record of her sister's findings.

But it wasn't anything quite as handy as that. A notation in the front declared the small book belonged to Matthew Fields. Flipping through the pages, Tess saw a record of musical engagements, dating back many years, with names and addresses, presumably of the other musicians and contacts, along with comments about each performance. She flipped to a date two months before. The appointments continued on for several weeks, but the comments ended.

Her dad hadn't been alive to perform, to comment, to plan ahead.

But three weeks after his death, the comments began again in a different handwriting along with records of coming engagements. And a name at the top of the page made Tess catch her breath.

Caroline Mays.

Her mother?

Caroline Mays was now the pianist taking the place of Matt Fields. Caroline Mays had to be the name Katie was currently using and she hadn't known the name existed until she read the letter after their father died.

Tess stared at the name for a long time before closing the book and looking to see what else she would find. Along with a bank book made out to Caroline Mays and a few other important papers that had been missing from the apartment, there was an Oregon driver's license made out to Katie Fields and another for Caroline Mays, a twenty-seven-year-old woman with bright-red hair and black frame glasses. Tess recalled the reddish hair at Katie's hairline, just visible under the bandages, hair that Tess had assumed was stained with blood from her injury. Not blood, hair dye.

What form had Katie's investigation taken? Who had she talked to, who had she worried to the point they tried to kill her? What was someone looking for when they tore her apartment apart? Had they found it? Why had Katie hidden her new ID along with her old one?

Tess picked up the little book again, turning to the date of Katie's hit-and-run and found a note about a birthday party for someone named Tabitha. Was she the young woman in the party hat? Seemed a reasonable possibility. A few days before that Katie had played Mozart at a place called Bluebird House. The very next day, she'd been scheduled to play there again. Beethoven's "Moonlight Sonata" this time.

Tess put everything back in the box and went in to talk to Ryan, but he was still asleep. She sat down on a kitchen chair and watched him for a while.

What was it about him that kept her staring? She knew lots of attractive men in San Francisco, men who weren't bossy and didn't carry guns. Men who laughed more, men who worried less, men whose past didn't seem to eat away at them.

She'd found none of those men interesting. This one she found fascinating and sexy and troublesome and didn't have the slightest insight into why.

Unless it was because he was so different from her.

In the middle of all this speculation, she suddenly recalled the items she'd put back in the cabinet under the bathroom sink. Jumping to her feet, she went to look, and sure enough, found the small box whose importance she'd overlooked before.

Mountain Sunrise the label said, showing a woman with brilliant red hair climbing a snow-covered peak at the break of dawn.

Tess stared at the box for a long time as a plan flitted and floated like a windblown leaf through her head, taking form and substance until it seemed the most reasonable, the most obvious plan she'd ever come up with.

And the most dangerous.

Chapter Four

Peter called Ryan's name.

Heart thumping wildly, Ryan ran through empty streets until he came to an old house, all the windows boarded up. Only the door stood open, a deep, black rectangle, gaping like a wound against the whitewashed planks.

Peter's voice came again…fainter…coming from inside…a hopeless pleading tone that set Ryan on fire.

Ignoring the door, Ryan attacked the windows one after the other. As his brother's voice receded, Ryan tore at the boards, fingers gouged by rusty nails, palms pierced by ragged splinters, blood dripping down his arms, splattering his chest. The last board from the last window came off, and he stood there panting. Every single window ended in solid wood—there were no openings. He turned back to the door—it was gone.

"Peter!" he yelled, and awoke with a start.

For a moment he lay there, unsure if he'd actually screamed, unsure where he was except that he felt stiff and out of sorts and there was a gun poking him in the rib cage. Full consciousness came back in a flash.

His gun. He'd fallen asleep in the chair without even taking off his gun.

The light peeking through Katie Fields's living room window confirmed it was likely to be another drizzly Oregon winter day. His eyes felt gritty, his back sore, his mood as dank and oppressive as the weather. Sometime during the night, someone had tossed a pink bedspread across his legs. His keen police instincts deduced he had Tess to thank for that.

Speaking of Tess… Disentangling himself from the pink quilt, he sat up and ran his hands through his hair. It was a small apartment and he could see the whole thing from his vantage point by the front door. Except for the bedroom, that was. He stared at the closed door, remembering the open door in his dream, the one he'd ignored until it was too late and it disappeared.

Getting to his feet and folding the unwieldy quilt, he fought a mounting desire to make sure Tess was still here. Tucking the quilt under one arm, he walked to the bedroom door and rapped loudly, calling her name. "Tess? May I come in?"

She didn't answer. He pushed open the door.

She'd finished cleaning up the room, rehung the curtains, remade the bed, put away clothes and shoes and books, had even found the cell-phone cord and plugged the small unit in on the nightstand to recharge its battery. The bed looked a little rumpled, the white blanket slightly mussed, a small depression in the plump pillow. He recalled Tess's theory that Katie had packed light and hadn't planned on living here long. As he surveyed the room with a practiced police eye, he had to agree. The Katie he recalled wouldn't live so austerely. There was an obvious lack of the usual feminine doodads one usually found cluttering every horizontal surface in a woman's bedroom.

A quick peek into the bathroom sent adrenaline pulsating through his body because it, too, was empty.

Tess was gone.

Once he'd dumped the quilt on the bed, he paced back into the living room, unsure where to start his search, scanning the apartment for signs of a struggle, chiding himself for sleeping through whatever had happened to get Tess out of this apartment without his knowledge. He pulled out his cell phone.

A noise in the hall drew his attention and he pocketed the phone and drew his gun in a series of fluid motions he barely thought about. He was at the door as it began a slow creep inward. Grabbing the knob, he pulled it fast. Tess came flying into his arms.

For a second she stared up at him, her blue eyes wide in surprise. One of his arms had looped around her back; he ignored his impulse to pull her into a full embrace.

She wore a black sweatshirt with the hood securely tied around her face. The hood and shoulders of the sweatshirt sparkled with raindrops. Her cheeks were rosy, giving her a fresh, country look.

"Do you have to point a gun at me *every* time we meet?" she said.

He dropped his arm and she moved away as he murmured, "Sorry," followed by an irate "Where have you been? What were you doing out there alone? How can I impress on you the fact that you might be in mortal danger? For an intelligent woman, you are the most stubborn—"

"Are you about finished?" Tess interrupted.

Actually, he was. He suspected the fact that he'd slept through Tess's departure was getting the better of him. That and the way she looked. And felt. A moment ago she'd been pressed against his chest, her body solid yet lithe, covered in cool, damp clothing beneath his heated hand, and he'd—

"Yeah, I'm finished," he said, taking a deep breath and tucking his gun away against the small of his back.

"I went to see Katie," she said calmly, unzipping her jacket. "There's been no change, by the way. Don't look so alarmed. I was careful. I covered my head and left through the door at the back of the apartment house, running along the beach for a while so no one could follow me, then doubling back. It's only a couple of miles over there. This is probably the last morning I'll be able to go outside the apartment without certain adjustments, so I took a chance and went."

"The last morning? Adjustments? I don't understand."

Carefully, staring right into his eyes, she pulled the hood back from her face, allowing her hair to tumble to her shoulders.

For a second he just stared at her, trying to figure out why in the world she would choose to dye her beautiful silky blond hair fire-engine red. And now? Why now? Had she gone nuts?

"Don't look at me like that," she said, slipping out of the sweatshirt. Beneath she wore a form-fitting white T-shirt with a deeply scooped neck. For the first time he was aware not only of her face and curvy waist and hips, but also of the gentle, soft slopes of her breasts. All the unsuitable feelings he'd had since waking collided in his gut and he looked away.

"I'm not crazy," she said.

He wasn't sure how to answer her. Not crazy for running around with a would-be killer on the prowl for her look-alike? Not crazy for changing her appearance? That must be it. Making a point of studying her red hair, he said, "I have to admit I like you as a blonde better, but this *is* different, this might confuse the issue. Still…"

His voice trailed off as she turned to walk into the bedroom and returned a moment later carrying a large paper shopping bag. She pulled from it a pair of black frame glasses that she perched on her nose, dwarfing her delicate features. "There's an all-night drugstore a couple of blocks over," she informed him as she handed him a small card.

"An all night—Tess, just how many times did you go in and out that blasted door?"

"I couldn't sleep and you seemed…restless. Anyway, look at what I handed you."

Lowering his gaze, he found himself staring at a driver's license that matched perfectly the seemingly nearsighted redhead standing in front of him.

Caroline Mays, it read.

"You didn't buy this at an all-night drugstore," he said sternly.

"No," she agreed. "I bought the glasses and a few supplies at the drugstore. The license I found hidden in a shoe box in Katie's bedroom."

"It looks like the kind issued by the state," he said uneasily as he turned it over.

"Doesn't it just scream possibilities?" she said.

He was beginning to get a bad feeling as he looked from it to Tess's face, all but masked by the glasses. She rustled in the sack for something else and emerged with a white object. Pulling her left pants leg up to her knee, she slipped what he realized was a cast over her foot and pulled it halfway up her shapely calf. "I made myself a walking cast," she said. "I know Katie's leg isn't broken, but the cast adds a degree of credibility to my costume, don't you think?"

The bad feeling intensified.

"Listen, Ryan," she said earnestly, "I think you're right, I think Katie was conducting her own investigation. She got herself a fake license, probably from someone she met while tending bar, quit her job, dyed her hair, moved into a strange part of town and put on a big old pair of glasses. The bad guys caught on to what she was up to and tried to kill her, so the Katie…I mean, Caroline…of today would need proof of an injury. Like a cast on the leg someone might have mentioned was injured in the 'accident.' I'll wrap my head in a bandage, too, and apply makeup to look like bruising—"

"Wait a second," he said, struggling to keep his voice down. She seemed surprised at the interruption.

"Yes?"

"You've bought yourself some big glasses, dyed your hair and made yourself a cast for what exact reason?"

She smiled. "Can't you guess, Ryan?"

"I'm afraid to guess," he told her truthfully.

"It's simple," she said, glancing away as though fearing censure. "To become my sister's alter ego, Caroline Mays. To find out what she found out, to discover who hurt her, to clear our father's name."

He was speechless.

She slipped off the cast and met his gaze again. "Come over here and sit down. Let me explain what I found last night. Let me tell you exactly what I plan to do."

She took his hand and led him to the kitchen. He wanted to believe he was too numb to register the feel of her cool hand on his, but her touch resounded up his arm despite his irritation with her naiveté. Thrusting yet another untimely reaction aside, he settled on anger. This woman was going to get in the middle of *his* investigation, she was sure to mess things up. She needed to back off and leave him to do what he needed to do and not play private investigator.

The rational part of him said he should try to reason with her in a sane, calm way.

The other nine-tenths wanted to throw her over his shoulder and deliver her to the airport where he would personally make sure she got on the first flight out of New Harbor.

Couldn't she see that pretending to be someone else had gotten her sister run over? Didn't she know that pretending to be someone pretending to be someone else was a recipe for disaster?

Where was that nice, quiet, sensible woman of the night before, the one who had agreed to go home, who had agreed to let him take charge of this mess?

He had the horrible feeling that if he didn't figure out a way to nip this recklessness in the bud, Tess Mays, aka Katie Fields, aka Caroline Mays, was going to get herself killed.

SOMETHING HAD HAPPENED to Tess during the night, and as she sat across from Ryan, she considered the best way to explain it to him.

As she regarded his unyielding expression and the smoldering intensity of his eyes, she knew she needed to make it concise, convincing and logical.

She asked him to stay where he was and went back into the bedroom to retrieve the shoe box. Returning to the kitchen, she set it on the table in front of him and took off the lid. Her sister's private treasure trove lay within. There was nothing terribly personal in the box, and she knew she needed help. She might have the power of her convictions, but she had no practical experience.

"What's this?" he asked, looking up at her as she moved to stand behind him. For a second she was distracted by the way a few dark, glossy hairs brushed the top of his shirt.

This was the first time she'd seen him without the leather jacket. The first time she'd seen the flat stomach, the biceps, the breadth of his shoulders covered with thin cotton. There wasn't an extra ounce of fat on the man; he obviously spent some time at a gym.

"Tess?"

"Huh? Oh, this is what I found in Katie's closet last night. Look in that little notebook on top."

"This?" He opened it and thumbed through the pages.

"It's a record of my father's musical engagements," she said. "Those handwritten notes are his at first, and then after his death, Katie's."

She pointed out what she meant, resting one hand on his solid shoulder and leaning forward, her hair sweeping his cheek.

"So what?" he said, turning his head to look at her as she leaned over his shoulder. This put them nose to nose, his eyes so close she could count his lashes, his mouth almost touching her chin.

She warned herself to stay businesslike. "Remember, Katie didn't know our mother's name until after our father died," she said. "The fact that she chose an alias for her work with the musical group must mean she suspected someone from Dad's music circle or the establishments he frequented was involved and she shouldn't use her own name. He played all over town, from the civic center to nursing homes and a place called Bluebird House. She must have figured someone in one of those places had information. Otherwise, Katie would have used her own name, right?"

"Maybe," Ryan agreed as Tess stood up, out of temptation's way. He turned around in the chair and pinned her with his gaze. "Or maybe her reasons for joining were purely sentimental. Maybe she just wanted to follow in his footsteps. Maybe she didn't want to be linked directly to him in case the people in the group or at one of the places they entertained had followed the news blitz following the fire. Or maybe they'd been questioned by the police concerning Matt Fields's whereabouts or connections. Perhaps they even felt a little threatened, as though they'd done something wrong or someone would think they had, the old guilt-by-association thing. Or maybe they were just disappointed that someone they knew and trusted violated his oath to serve and protect and instead plotted arson and murder."

His remarks hit her like a slap in the face, way out of proportion, considering the only thing she knew about her father was that he'd walked away from her when she was an infant and never, it seemed, looked back.

That's not true, she argued with herself. *During this night you've come to know him through Katie's eyes. And Katie's eyes are your eyes in a way, aren't they?*

He was Katie's dad and he was your dad. You believe in his innocence.

"Tess?"

"I think you're projecting your own sense of betrayal with my father on this issue," she said softly, moving deeper into the living area, further from him, perching at last on the edge of the coffee table. She took off the glasses and set them beside her, lining the lenses up with the grain of the wood. "I'm going to keep the appointment Katie made to play 'Moonlight Sonata' this morning at Bluebird House," she said softly, staring at the glasses and not at Ryan. "I've played the piano for years. My mother hated hearing me practice—I guess it reminded her of my father—but I was driven to play. Maybe someone there can explain—"

"Where you left your brain?" he snapped, standing. He shook the notebook at her. "This is ridiculous."

That got her attention. "No it's not."

"Try to remember that I actually *know* your sister. You've built some pie-in-the-sky image of her as an intrepid crusader—"

Tess almost tipped over the table as she, too, shot to her feet, the glasses sliding to the carpet. "Don't you dare talk about her like that," she said. "I do know Katie. I got to know her during the night. I touched her things, I lay in her bed, I put on her clothes." She didn't add the rest because she knew he would scoff at it. The truth was that sometime in the middle of the night after dying her hair and reaching certain conclusions, she'd peered into Katie's mirror and seen a reflection different from the one she expected. And it wasn't just the hair color, either, it was something in the eyes. Tess felt empowered by her sister's essence, though that didn't explain it, not really.

She just knew she wasn't afraid anymore.

"And now you're determined to turn into her," Ryan said. "You're as reckless as she is."

She stepped backward and heard the crunch of the glasses as she trod on them. Too upset to care, she tossed her head defiantly. "Thanks."

"It wasn't meant as a compliment," he snarled. He looked down at his feet—was he counting to ten?—then back at her. "Tess, Tess. How are you going to explain the fact that you don't know the people Katie knows or have her memories?"

She tried one last time to enlist his aid by demonstrating she'd thought this through. "In case whomever did this is at Bluebird House or is watching the apartment, from now on I'll wear glasses and bandages and the walking cast. I mean, they're bound to know they hit me, so I'll give them what they might expect to see. A minor break in my leg, bruises, bandages around my head. I'll blame any memory lapses or confusion on the mild concussion I suffered. I'll make sure everyone hears me say I have no idea what happened. I'll misdirect them by saying the police are looking for a green SUV or a red truck from out of state. Katie will be safer, the would-be killer can relax, I can sniff out possibilities."

Ryan rubbed the back of his neck as he sat down in his chair. "When you say *Katie* will be safer, you do realize that in this context, for all intents and purposes, you are talking about yourself, not your sister?" he said. "Your *sister* is all tucked away in ICU behind locked doors. By going out and pretending to be her you are anything but safer. You do know that, don't you?"

She said, "Yes. That's why I need your help."

She thought he would protest again or maybe even stalk out of the apartment. He said, "You're going to do this with or without me, aren't you?"

Surprised, she whispered, "Yes."

"When are you supposed to be at the Bluebird House?"

"In two hours."

He stood again and walked right up to her, forcing her to look up at him. "You know I don't approve of this scheme?"

"Yes."

"And you'll be cautious? You'll keep me posted, you won't go off on some tangent without checking in? I'll allow you to be my partner, but the trade-off is you have to keep me as yours. Okay?"

"Okay."

"I'm going to regret this," he said.

"No you won't. Go home and freshen up."

"I'm not leaving you alone in this apartment until we get that door fixed," he said.

Tess moved away from him, breathing easier when she'd put a couple of feet between them. For a second, as he stood looking down at her and she up at him, they'd been close enough that his body heat hit her full force and she'd had to caution herself not to succumb to the comfort of his arms...and not because of fear this time.

She dug back into her shopping bag. "I thought you might refuse to leave," she told him, "so I bought you some new underwear at the drugstore and a toothbrush and some deodorant and even a new white T-shirt. You can shower here. If you want."

He stared at her, and she wondered if it was bad form to buy black briefs for a man you'd known less than forty-eight hours. Too late if it was. "I took a guess at the size," she added, "and, um, the style."

He accepted the plastic-wrapped items with a look of disbelief still on his face. "I miss the reasonable veterinarian of yesterday," he muttered, meeting her gaze.

"Yeah, well, she's gone for now," Tess said.

"I can see that," he told her, and strode off toward the bathroom.

HE DROVE HER to Bluebird House with one eye on the road and one eye on the rearview mirror. He'd never in his life been so damn aware of a woman; the third eye he'd developed was glued to her.

She wore the small turquoise earrings and ring he had dumped out of the evidence bag the night before, along with an inexpensive white dress she'd found in Katie's closet. Her new red tresses brushed her shoulders, her new black glasses perched on her nose.

What the glasses didn't obscure, the bandages wrapped around her head did. There was a smudge of dried blood on one edge, discreet, barely noticeable, but a nice touch. She'd also come up with a black eye for herself and had put on a loose, long-sleeved sweater to cover her arms. The cast looked real, and they'd picked up a pair of aluminum crutches to emphasize her injury when they'd stopped to replace the glasses.

She didn't look much like the smartly dressed blonde veterinarian he'd first met three days before. She didn't look much like Katie, either, which was the point.

She also didn't look as frightened as she should be, but warning her seemed pointless. He'd already tried. Perhaps, he thought, she was more focused than scared, and how could he fault her for that? It was the police credo.

"How far away are we?" she asked, her voice the only part of her that revealed a show of nerves.

"Not far." He sent her a hurried glance as the light turned green. He said, "Tess, when I first joined the New Harbor Police Force I worked undercover. For three months I wore the same ratty clothes and spent most of my nights on the street buying and selling drugs, trying to work my way up to meet the sleaze-ball in charge. I called myself Brian. Just Brian. Notice how close it is to Ryan. It's a old undercover trick—choose a name that sounds like your own so you won't be startled or fail to answer when someone addresses you."

He could feel her staring at him.

"Pretending to be someone else takes concentration," he continued. "You have an edge because you're basically playing your doppelganger, but you aren't Tess Mays anymore, you're Katie Fields, but damn it, you aren't even Katie Fields, you're Caroline Mays. Get use to the name Caroline."

"You're forgetting that Caroline Mays is my mother. I've grown up with that name. If Katie could be Caroline, I can be Caroline."

"But Katie didn't know her mother, so Katie was no doubt being Katie with a new name and red hair."

"So tell me what I need to know about Katie."

He shook his head. "Well, pretty, of course, but a little flighty for my taste and besides, she was Matt's daughter."

"What does that mean?"

"You don't mess around with a partner's daughter."

"Is this police code?"

"No, this is common sense. I think Matt wanted her married and settled down, or at least educated, but after a couple of years of junior college she dropped out. I don't think she could afford to go anymore. Matt never had extra money to help her. Well, we now know why—he was too busy gambling it away. And Katie mostly did odd jobs like bartending, which I gather she was good at. She likes people. Other than that, I don't know what to tell you."

Tess was so quiet he glanced her way. He found she'd scrolled through the photos on the phone until she'd found the one of her sister and father and was staring at it. Biting her lip, she stuck the phone in his glove box. "I'm not taking any chances that some friend of Katie's chooses the wrong moment to call. Okay, it sounds as though Katie is outgoing. I'm not so good with people. Much better with animals. I'll pretend everyone at Bluebird House is a dog or a cat."

Ryan cast her a worried frown. "Do me a favor," he said, his hands gripping the wheel.

"Instead of pretending everyone at Bluebird House is a nice cuddly pet, pretend they're a cold-blooded killer."

Chapter Five

A brochure inside the door informed Tess that Bluebird House catered to developmentally disabled adults with or without physical limitations. The room Tess was shown to was set up wedding style for the occasion, the white baby grand piano situated at the front. Tess felt a flutter of nerves as she recalled just how long it had been since she'd actually played "Moonlight Sonata."

The staff was alternately horrified and curious about her injuries, as were the two other musicians, one a middle-aged dentist/violinist, and the other a retired banker who could play any number of instruments. Tess was by necessity vague during their brief conversation, touching her forehead often to drive home the point that she'd suffered a minor concussion and couldn't remember nine-tenths of the things they talked about. They seemed to grow bored with her very quickly, which was a relief. They'd both been checked out after the fire; Ryan had said not to waste too much time on them or any of the other members of the troupe who hadn't been scheduled for this day's activity.

As far as their audience went, there were about forty people present, mostly residents though members of the staff were clearly in evidence, as well. Tess kept her eyes peeled for the girl on Katie's phone. She had a gut feeling this person was important to Katie, and hopefully, to the investigation, as well. Surely she must be connected to Bluebird House in some way.

Despite Tess's occasional fumbles, which she hoped were attributed to her injuries, the recital was well received. When the last notes faded away, followed by enthusiastic clapping, a woman wearing a smock announced refreshments in the dining room.

As people filed out haphazardly, sweeping the other two musicians in their wake, Tess imagined her father doing this for years. He had apparently been both a gambler and a volunteer musician; such an odd combination, one interest so selfish, the other so selfless.

And then Katie followed in his path, a "people person" Ryan had called her. Tess felt a renewed connection to this twin sister she didn't know and a renewed jab of anger with her mother for keeping them apart.

Which brought up the burning question: where was her mother? Every time Tess placed a call, her mother's phone switched to voice mail yet she hadn't returned one of Tess's increasingly demanding missives. And what about her new husband's stepson? Never available, never even home, according to his housekeeper. Who was this man and why was he avoiding her? What kind of family had her mother married into?

Tess was awkwardly gathering up her music when someone tugged at her sleeve. She turned to find a girl just out of her teens with a pale, round face, blue eyes, curly reddish-blond hair, wearing a green jogging suit with flower embroidery. As short as Tess was, this girl was shorter, barely reaching Tess's shoulder.

"Caroline," the girl said, struggling to make herself understood. A tad cross-eyed, she had a deep lisp that blurred the syllables making "Caroline" sound like "Carewine."

"Hello," Tess said, recognizing at once the girl on Katie's phone. She wore a name tag that read Tabitha Woodall. The name seemed familiar. "Did you like the music?" she asked.

The girl nodded enthusiastically. "Nice," she said and in a pleasant sing-song way added, "Tanks for kitty."

For kitty. What kitty? Tess looked up as a gray-haired woman in a tailored black suit approached, hazel eyes wide with shock. "Oh, my gosh, Caroline, I just heard! A hit-and-run accident!"

"I'm fine," Tess said as the woman gripped her hand.

"Did it happen right after you left my house Tuesday?" Lowering her voice, she added, "Were you able to keep your appointment with Nelson Lingford?"

"I...I don't know," Tess said, her confusion disguising the sudden constriction in her chest. "I'm a little fuzzy on details," she added. *Katie had had an appointment with Nelson Lingford the very same day she was hit and left to die?* Here was something Ryan didn't know!

"This is just dreadful," the woman continued.

"Tank for kitty," the girl repeated, frustration twisting her blunt features. "At da party, da kitty."

The older woman said, "Yes, yes, Tabitha." Glancing back at Tess, she added, "My daughter just loves the kitty you gave her."

The girl smiled, took the older woman's hand and put it to her cheek.

Mother and daughter? No two women looked less alike than these two, one short and round, forever young, with guileless transparent eyes, the other tall and angular, middle sixties, intelligence burning behind her gaze. Tess tried her best to look as if she knew what they were talking about. She finally noticed the tiny silver cat hanging from a green ribbon around Tabitha's neck.

"I'm so glad you like the kitty," Tess said.

"Pretty," Tabitha said, fingering her pendant.

"After you left Tabitha's little birthday bash, I drove her back here," the woman added. "It doesn't pay to overstimulate her, as you know, and she was getting so tired. I'm sorry, by the way, she got so excited when you took her picture. I thought she was going to break your little phone. You'll tell me if I need to replace it, won't you?"

"She didn't hurt it," Tess said.

"I like da picture," Tabitha said. "I see?"

"I'm sorry, I don't have the phone with me, Tabitha. "Next time, okay?"

Tabitha clapped her hands together. Tess wasn't sure what that meant, but in the next moment, the girl grabbed Tess, stepping on her foot in the process. Tess swallowed a wince and returned the hug. The genuine emotion prompting the girl's action spoke volumes about Katie's ability to communicate with all kinds of people, and Tess was oddly proud of her twin sister.

Gently disengaging her daughter, the mother said, "Careful, sweetheart. Go along now and get yourself a cookie. I'll be there in a moment."

Tabitha reluctantly released Tess from her strangle-hold and went in search of cookies as the woman fetched Tess's crutches from where she'd stacked them against a wall. "Do you really feel up to keeping your appointment with Madeline Lingford today?" she asked over her shoulder.

Tess allowed herself a befuddled expression as she fitted the crutches beneath her arms. An appointment with Madeline Lingford? Would she refuse such an opportunity? Not likely. She said, "Of course. Do you happen to know when she's expecting me?"

"Anytime. I'm on my way over to her place after I eat a cookie with Tabitha. You can't drive, can you? Shall I give you a lift?"

Pausing a moment to think of Ryan waiting outside, Tess grabbed the opportunity and said, "That would be great."

RYAN SPENT most of the time Tess was inside Bluebird House scrolling through Katie's cell phone, looking for something he might have missed. A number, a contact, a name... anything. He found nothing.

He was just throwing it back in the glove box when Tess hobbled out the big front doors, accompanied by an older woman in a gray raincoat. Neither Tess or the stranger gave him a second glance as they proceeded to a small black car. He could barely believe his eyes when Tess got into the passenger seat, pulling her crutches in behind her.

He hit the steering wheel. That woman had been working undercover less than three hours and already she was breaking the rules!

The trouble with being shut out of the investigation after Tess's father died was that now he didn't know many of the suspects by sight. He'd have to identify the woman Tess left with by running her automobile plates, which he did as he trailed her car out of the parking lot.

The ID came back: Irene Sarah Woodall. He recognized the name as being connected to the Lingford family. She was an art dealer. That was it. Her home address was in the opposite direction from where she was driving and she was no slouch when it came to speed. He stayed as far back as he could, wishing there were more cars on the road, feeling conspicuous as they headed out of town.

The land south of the New Harbor had consisted mostly of sand dunes and small lakes until fifteen years before when Nelson Lingford, as part of a consortium, bought up every last acre and began an "improvement" plan, transforming it all into pricey real estate. Now it housed a country club, two golf courses and huge, elaborate estates. Rocking Sand Road was one of the addresses located closest to the ocean, a winding lane bordered by dunes on one side and fir trees on the other. Gated fences kept out the riffraff.

Did Tess have the slightest idea what she was getting herself into?

TESS STARED OUT her window but saw very little as her racing thoughts blurred the outside world. Why did Madeline Lingford want to see her?

Obviously, Katie had arranged this meeting before her "accident." She must have been onto something. She sent a message winging to her sister's subconscious: *Katie, wake up, I need answers.*

She resolutely put Katie out of her mind. Turning her gaze to Irene Woodall, she said, "Tabitha is a doll."

"How sweet of you to say. I had her rather late in life. Unfortunately, my husband died when she was only seven. Due to the physical problems Tabitha faces, as well as the developmental ones, she's had to live away from home for several years now. She's prone to temper tantrums, but you know that. I can't tell you how difficult it is to have a child you know will never grow up, never grow old."

"Never grow old?"

"Her heart," Irene said, her voice heavy. "I'll be lucky to have her another five years."

"I'm so sorry. I imagine you've told me most of this before."

Irene nodded. "Most of it."

"It's this blasted concussion. Not bad enough to keep me down, just bad enough to scramble my short-term memory. Or did we know each other from long ago—"

"Oh, no. I just met you a few weeks ago when you played at Bluebird House for the first time. Tabitha liked you immediately."

"And how did I come to meet the Lingfords?"

"I introduced you. Nelson Lingford had just bought a piano and wanted someone with experience to give his stepmother a couple of lessons. I've known Madeline Lingford for years. We became widows about the same time. I don't personally think she gives a fig about piano lessons, but as you know, what Nelson wants, Nelson usually gets. Anyway, Madeline tries to indulge him. You and Nelson hit it off and there you go, here we are."

"And you?"

"I own an art gallery. I used to help Madeline's late husband acquire art from around the world. He had a wonderful collection."

"I vaguely remember that the man accused of setting the fire died in the fire, right?"

Irene nodded. "Yes, he was the same man who played the piano before you! But I don't think he was really involved. I think he's been used as a scapegoat. I believe I mentioned this to you before—"

"So many blurred details," Tess mumbled. Did this woman have proof of their father's innocence? Was that why Katie had tried to call Ryan? "Tell me what we talked about last Tuesday," she said.

The art dealer spared Tess a longer glance. "You don't recall anything?"

"Not a word."

"Well, mostly it was a party for Tabitha so we didn't talk much. I do know the last thing you asked from me was that I ask Madeline's maid for the names of any employees Nelson let go near the time of the fire."

"I wonder why I wanted them," Tess mused.

"Well, you told me you'd heard the rumors about Nelson and the fire. Frankly, I had the impression you wanted to make sure Nelson's not an out-and-out crook before things went any further between you."

"Between us?"

Irene spared her another glance. "Don't be embarrassed. I understand how a wealthy man like Nelson Lingford could turn a woman's head. I was young once, too. But I'll tell you now what I told you before. Be careful. You never know what Nelson is really thinking."

Was it possible Katie's investigation had nothing to do with clearing their father and everything to do with catching a rich husband?

Using an assumed identity? No. Of course not.

Tess said, "I'm remembering a name now. Desota. A friend of Nelson's?"

This earned her a sharp look. "Vince and Nelson are hardly friends anymore," Irene said, pulling up to a locked gate.

As her window glided down, she gave her name to an intercom and the gate swung open. The road ended in a circular drive in front of a mammoth two-story house.

"Mrs. Lingford's new house is beautiful," Tess said.

"No, no, this is Nelson's house. After the fire gutted Madeline's place, he moved her in with him to keep an eye on her."

"That…that was kind of him," Tess stammered. She hadn't realized she was going to Nelson's house. She had to fight the impulse to turn in her seat to make sure Ryan was back there somewhere.

Irene stopped beside a shabby car that looked totally out of place. Ignoring it, she turned in her seat to stare into Tess's eyes. "You're way too trusting, Caroline. Please, watch your step with Nelson. He's hiding something, I can feel it in my bones."

THE OVERSIZE FRONT DOOR closed with a resounding thud as an honest-to-goodness maid took their coats and looked askance at Tess's crutches as though afraid the rubber tips might smudge the polished cherry floors.

"Tell Mrs. Lingford that Caroline Mays is here," Irene said as she shed her coat and helped Tess with hers. The entry, like the rest of what Tess could see of the house, was decorated to within an inch of its life with perfectly coordinated fabrics, wall coverings, and furniture. There was even an elevator with a brass-grill overlay. It looked like the lobby of a small but swanky hotel.

The peaceful luxury was shattered as a door to the left burst open and a short man with a ring of dark hair appeared. Dressed in a rumpled gray suit too large for him, he was sweating profusely. He wiped his high forehead with a handkerchief as his gaze swept over Tess and Irene. He didn't seem to really see them at all.

He was followed out of the room by another man who was probably close in age, but that's where all comparisons ended. This man was tanned and sandy-haired with a sun-bleached mustache, dressed in dark slacks, a cashmere jacket and a white turtle-neck setting off his bronze skin.

"Don't you ever come back here again," the second man snarled, his focus centered on the first man.

"You owe me and you know it!" the balding man said, stuffing his handkerchief into his jacket pocket. He had down-on-his-luck written all over him.

"Get out of my house," the tanned man said in a menacing tone.

"I trusted you," the first man said. "I mortgaged my business. You promised me—"

"I never promised you a thing. You were greedy, Vince. You've always been greedy ever since high school. This time it bit you in the ass."

"Darla left me," Vince said. "Took the kids and went to her mother's. My business is in the toilet. The creditors, the bank. Hell, the police are coming around all the time asking questions…"

Nelson's expression went from irritated to furious. "If I ever find out you were behind that fire—"

"Who are you trying to kid?" Vince Desota spat. "We all know—"

"Get out!" Nelson said, and this time he accompanied his demand with advancing steps.

Desota scooted backward, his gaze finally taking in Tess, who he stared at with puzzled eyes before yanking open the door and leaving the house.

For a moment only the ticking of a big clock broke the silence. Nelson straightened his jacket and smoothed his lapels, though the altercation hadn't seemed to ruffle more than his temper. Tires peeled on the driveway as he said, "I'm sorry you two ladies had to witness that."

Irene shook her head. "What did Vince want?"

"Money, what else?" He looked at Tess more closely and his eyes narrowed. "Good heavens, Caroline, what happened to you?"

"She was in an accident, but she still insisted on coming to give Madeline a piano lesson," Irene said. It was obvious to Tess that Katie had cultivated a confidante within the Lingford household in the form of Irene Woodall. Tess had to figure out a way to get rid of Irene if she didn't want the older woman getting in her way. "And I'm here, as usual, to help Madeline correlate the photos for her album," Irene added.

"I wish you'd get her to make it into a book. That at least would find a market, even if a small one. Well, at least this album is keeping her busy. She doesn't seem interested in the blasted piano I spent a fortune on." Approaching Tess he added, "Were you injured after we met last Tuesday?"

So he and Katie had met. What had they talked about?

"Caroline?"

"It's my memory," she explained. "I don't recall the day of the accident. The police think a teenage driver is responsible." She liked the touch of the teenager. So easy to blame them for things. No one ever disagreed.

"Damn thugs," Nelson sniffed.

The maid reappeared. "Ms. Madeline will see you in the music room," she said.

"I'll just go upstairs and fetch the photos," Irene said with a meaningful glance at Tess.

She hoped Irene was going to get the names she'd mentioned.

IN RYAN'S EXPERIENCE no plan ever went off without a hitch. He faced his current hitch, a giant iron gate including an intercom box and a camera mounted ona post.

The rain had begun again in earnest, and he weighed his options as the windshield wipers banged back and forth. He could climb the gate and hope the camera wasn't turned on; skirt the perimeter and look for an opening, probably on the ocean side; punch the intercom button and announce himself, using the cousin-with-a-ride story they'd agreed on for the Bluebird House and which she'd promptly abandoned.

Or he could wait.

He hated waiting.

Since making detective three years before, he'd had to get used to it. Back when he was a beat cop, he could go find something to do if he got bored, but now he was duty-bound to sit and twiddle his thumbs for hours. Waiting.

Fifteen minutes, thirty tops.

He'd wait despite the acid churning in his stomach, despite the dread that if he waited too long, someone would die because of him. It was a specter that had haunted him his entire career, but he made himself sit and he made himself wait.

Despite the risk.

Despite what had happened to Peter because Ryan had waited.

MADELINE LINGFORD sat in a wheelchair, a brown lap blanket thrown across her knees. A spare woman with regular features and white poodle curls, her eyes looked friendly behind the thick lenses of her red glasses. The smile she produced for Tess slid off her face at the sight of the crutches and bandages.

This room, too, was beautifully decorated, though it was obviously the room Madeline had commandeered since moving in. She'd covered every surface with curios and memorabilia. It looked homey to Tess. It was also located far away from the entry. Tess thought it unlikely Madeline had heard a word of Nelson's altercation with Vince Desota.

After a new round of exclamations concerning Tess's injuries, Madeline gestured at the piano and said, "Nelson bought that thing. Said I needed a hobby. Something cultivated, though he didn't add that part. He thinks I'm a bit too ordinary to be a Lingford."

Tess smiled. Madeline Lingford was not the sickly invalid she'd expected to find. Nor was she snooty.

"So the good news for me is you don't look well enough to teach me piano, at least not today! Hallelujah. Sit down and talk to me. It gets lonely way out here in the middle of nowhere. I miss my house in the city."

A pang of guilt creased Tess's brow. Would this woman want her company if she knew it was Tess's own father who was accused of destroying her house? She sat on a sofa at a right angle to Madeline's wheelchair, surprised to find two coal-black eyes staring at her from within the folds of the lap blanket.

"Is that a dog?" she asked, smiling.

"This is Muffy," the older woman said, uncovering her pet. Muffy appeared to be fifteen pounds of terrier with coarse brown and black fur.

"She's adorable," Tess said, reaching out a finger any normal dog would sniff. This dog didn't move a corpuscle. She regarded Tess with dull brown eyes. "Is she not feeling well?"

"It's funny you should ask," Madeline said as Tess casually palpated the dog's neck and abdomen, attempting to make it appear she was only petting Muffy and not checking for swollen lymph nodes. "I was just telling Nelson this morning that Muffy hasn't been her usual bouncy self for a day or two now."

"Feeling a little under the weather, sweetie?" Tess crooned to the dog. Changing her tone, she asked Madeline, "Does she have her usual appetite?" and fingered back a lip to peer at Muffy's gums. Pale.

"No. Cook said she isn't eating a thing. And normally she's a little chow hound, aren't you, Muffy? But lately she just lies here."

Muffy seemed to make a slight effort to gaze up at her mistress but abandoned it in favor of resting her head back on her paws.

Tess wished she had a thermometer. She touched Muffy's nose, a notoriously poor indicator of a fever, but what else could she do? Dry and warm. Moreover, the animal had the look of sickness and a gut feeling gave way to certainty: something was wrong with Muffy.

"Have you kept up her vaccinations?" Tess asked.

"Of course. She's been my dearest friend for years, in fact, she saved my life a couple of months ago when my house burned down. Muffy's barking woke me up in time to call for help."

"Have you thought of taking her to the vet?"

"When she wouldn't eat, I asked Nelson, but he said she's getting old. We have to expect this kind of thing."

"How old is she?"

"Six."

"That's not old for a small terrier mix like Muffy," Tess said firmly, carving another notch next to Nelson Lingford's name in the villain column. Was it possible he blamed the dog for his stepmother's survival?

As Madeline rambled on, Tess reviewed the dog's symptoms in her mind. The most obvious choice was canine distemper, but this dog had had her shots. The other candidate seemed less likely, but this was the Pacific Northwest…

"Does she like fish?" Tess asked, again striving to sound casual.

"I give her canned albacore sometimes,"

Madeline said. "She likes that. Only, she won't eat it now. She won't eat any of her treats, not even the smoked steelhead Nelson started giving her last week. Oh, but she loved it at first."

Canned albacore, no. Smoked Steelhead? It must have been cold smoked. "Was last week the first time Muffy ate the steelhead?"

Madeline considered. "I think so. Nelson made a point of sharing it with her."

The veterinarian in Tess surpassed the spy as she calculated dates. If the dog had first ingested the fish the week before, the neorickettsia organism would have had plenty of time to start wreaking havoc.

"I think you should have Muffy checked for salmon poisoning," Tess said gently.

Madeline Lingford gasped audibly.

Tess touched the older woman's arm as she leaned forward. "Take her to the vet this afternoon. They'll give her fluids and antibiotics and she'll be good as new. It's not really poison at all, it's caused by a viruslike organism. The symptoms are exactly like Muffy's."

"I'll call right away," Madeline said, her voice shaky, her fingers already jabbing at numbers on the phone.

"I didn't realize you were such an animal expert."

Startled, Tess looked up. Nelson Lingford leaned elegantly in the doorway, his expression perplexed as he stared at her. How much had he heard? How professional had she sounded?

Well, as far as Tess could tell, there was no way for Nelson to know what Katie or "Caroline," for that matter, was or wasn't good at. She said, "I've had a lot of pets."

"Hmm—"

"The vet said to bring her in an hour," Madeline said, hugging her pup. "Oh, Caroline, I'm so grateful to you."

"I'm happy I could help," Tess said.

"I'll get the driver to give you a ride," Nelson said. "Meanwhile I came to borrow Caroline for a few moments. I need to…talk to her."

"Wait a second," Madeline said. "I've decided to postpone piano lessons, because I have a better idea. Caroline is so clever, I just know she could be a great deal of help organizing the photos of your father's collection. I feel guilty taking so much of Irene's time."

"My time?" Irene said, carrying two boxes past Nelson. They were clearly marked Photographs.

As Irene deposited the boxes on a table, Madeline explained Muffy's illness and her idea to hire Tess. Irene darted Tess a worried glance. "I don't know if that's a good idea," she said. "I mean, I'm happy to help you, Madeline, we don't need to take Caroline's time—"

"I can't have your gallery failing because you're over here all the time," Madeline insisted. "I thought at first Georges would help me out—"

"He's been so busy in the shop—"

"Exactly. And that's where you should be too, dear. You shouldn't leave your business in Georges's hands no matter how capable an assistant he is."

"I have to agree with Madeline," Nelson said.

Tess glanced at Irene. The older woman's eyes pleaded with Tess to refuse this offer. Would Katie have forged ahead or taken Irene's counsel? Who knew? Tess squared her shoulders and said, "I'd love the job."

"Then it's all settled," Madeline said. "Oh, Caroline, I wish you could have seen the real paintings. I had such a beautiful house in which to show them, didn't I, Nelson?"

"Father's mansion was exquisite. I still

can't understand how you could bear to part with his art."

"It was your father's last wish," she said firmly, as though this was an often-revisited topic. "Caroline, dear, thank you for saving Muffy."

Irene sidled close as Tess patted the dog's head. When Tess straightened, Irene slipped a strip of paper into her hand and gave her a worried look. Turning to Madeline, she said, "What's this about saving Muffy?"

"Caroline is a whiz," Madeline said. "I'll tell you all about it."

Nelson said, "Caroline? Would you step into my office for a moment?"

Tess stuffed the note in her pocket and followed him from the room.

Chapter Six

Tess paused right inside the door of Nelson's study to admire a row of framed photos of buildings.

"Some of my holdings," Nelson said.

It looked as though he owned most of New Harbor. Tess turned and found him standing closer than she expected. "I think I can understand why you hated having your father's art given away to the museum," she said, backing up a little. "They'd look wonderful hanging on your walls."

"I don't need more decorations on my walls," he said. "The collection was worth a small fortune. It was an investment. When Irene told me what Madeline had in mind, I was stunned. But legally it all belonged to my stepmother to do with as she wished. Trust me, I double-checked."

"The art itself—"

"Was beautiful, of course. And now most of it is gone, and what remains will soon be hanging on the museum walls in a room named after my father. Part of the deal, though now, of course, it can be a much smaller room than before. Meanwhile, I have plenty to keep me busy."

"Your investments," she mused.

He gestured at another row of photos, this of a man windsurfing. "This is my new passion. Wonderful sport," he said. "Man against nature. I've a trip planned for Hawaii later this month."

Tess hobbled over to the window located behind Nelson's desk to admire the magnificent view that included miles of rolling dunes, straight beaches, line upon line of gentle waves, a vast sky overhead, all of it tinted a million shades of bluish gray. For a moment she could almost see herself walking alone on the sand, and instantly her imagination provided an escort, a tall man with black hair whose head dipped close to hers.

Reality came back with a bang as she felt movement behind her. The next thing she knew, Nelson had wrapped one arm around her from behind, parted her hair, and pressed his lips against the back of her neck.

She was so stunned she couldn't think.

"Play your cards right and you can go with me to Maui," Nelson whispered.

In that instant another movement caught Tess's attention, this one coming from outside the window. A man suddenly appeared, raindrops spattering his glossy black hair, running down his face, glistening on his lashes. He looked in the window, apparently saw Tess, started to smile and then opened his mouth in shock.

Ryan!

For a second they stared into each other's eyes, then he disappeared around a corner.

Nelson kissed her again. His grip around her waist tightened. "Turn around and let me kiss you properly," he murmured.

She turned around all right, but put her hand over his mouth as he lunged toward her.

"I'm sorry," she said, dropping her hand. "This isn't a good time." Was Ryan still out there looking in?

"You *are* different today," Nelson allowed. "You haven't asked me a million questions like usual. I suppose I have your brush with death to thank?"

His phrasing made her jump. "Yes," she said, briefly meeting his intense gaze. "That and Muffy. Your stepmother is very upset."

"My stepmother is crazy about that un-pedigreed mutt."

Tess wanted to move away from him, but she didn't. It would be a shame to waste Katie's obvious efforts to seduce the truth out of Nelson just because she didn't like him. "Tell me what we talked about on Tuesday," she said, running a hand up and down his cashmere-covered arm, trying her best to look flirtatious. She wasn't good at this kind of thing. Her life had given her few opportunities to toy with men, and it didn't come naturally.

His lips twisted into a smile. He stared at the bandage wrapping her head. Had it slipped?

"You asked me about my stepmother's house fire," he said. "You seemed fascinated by the details."

"Which details?" Tess murmured as she touched her bandages. They felt okay.

He leaned closer. "The details concerning me," he said without elaborating.

"I just find you so fascinating," she gushed. "Did I come here to your house or did you come to mine?"

He laughed. "Caroline, what are you playing at? You know you won't tell me where you live. You came to my downtown office. You took a picture of my newest windsurfing trophy with your phone, then left like a shot."

The trophy on the phone! "Was I upset?"

He shrugged. "Hard to tell with you, isn't it? Plus, I got a call from Vince. I was a little preoccupied afterward—that jerk's whining is getting to me."

"He seemed so angry today—"

"He thinks I owe him every penny he lost. His life is spiraling away, and all he can do is blame me."

"And are you to blame?" she asked breathlessly.

"Hell, no! He begged me to get in on the Parkinson land deal. I warned him it depended on zoning. Is it my fault the commissioners had a sudden attack of conscience or that Vince mortgaged his business up the wazoo?" He narrowed his eyes and added, "What's with all these questions? Sometimes I wonder if you and Vince are—"

Just then a loud knock sounded on the outside door followed by several rings of the doorbell and the scurrying feet of the maid.

Tess recognized the loud male voice coming from the entry. Cursing Ryan under her breath, she tried to think of a way to draw Nelson's attention back to their conversation, but the moment was lost. He strode over to the door, opening it wide and addressing the commotion out in the entry. She followed him from the room.

"HE WAS RIGHT ON THE VERGE of accusing me of working for Vince Desota," she said a few moments later as she climbed into Ryan's car. "You ruined everything!"

Ryan gave her a quick look. After he'd gone into his cousin-come-to-give-a-ride act, the Lingfords had consented to open the gate to allow him to drive up to the house so Tess wouldn't have to walk the long driveway wielding cast and crutches, dodging raindrops and puddles. They couldn't understand why he hadn't used the intercom. He said he hadn't seen an intercom. He said someone at Bluebird House had told him Caroline left with Irene Woodall and that Irene Woodall had mentioned coming to the Lingfords. He was just a simple guy trying to take care of his cousin.

"Why did you come after me?" Tess

fussed as they drove back into town. "That wasn't part of the plan."

"We agreed you wouldn't go off on a tangent without me, and you did," he said, scathingly. His excursion around the Lingford house had left him dripping wet. It didn't distract from his looks. In fact, it made him even sexier. Easy to imagine what he would look like coming out of the shower, for instance. Her gut reaction to his half-drowned state just made her more angry.

"Are you honestly referring to an interrogation of Nelson and Madeline Lingford as a 'tangent'?"

"And I suppose it was part of the 'interrogation' to make out with your favorite suspect?"

"Make out? You call that making out?"

"Well what would you call it? It looked pretty cozy."

"Tell me you're not this dense."

He said nothing, but she saw a knot in his jaw that said plenty. For some reason it reminded her of the names Irene had slipped to her, and she dug in her sweater pocket.

"Do you suppose you could put this irrational attitude of yours aside for a second and answer a question?"

"I might be able to."

"Good." Reading from the paper, she said, "Do the names Jim Kinsey and Clint Doyle mean anything to you?"

It took him a moment to answer. "Former Lingford employees. Why?"

"Katie must have wanted these names for a reason. Apparently she visited Irene and her daughter on the morning of her accident. Afterward she went to Nelson's downtown office to discuss piano lessons for his stepmother. According to him, Katie asked a lot of questions. He got a phone call from Vince Desota that upset him, and I guess while he was on the phone, she used her cell phone to take a photo of his latest windsurfing trophy. Right after that, she took off. We know she started home, tried to call you, got hit by a white van."

"Good work," he said, but the knot was still in his jaw.

"Today Desota was at Nelson's house when we got there. The two of them were really going at it." She did her best to recount the conversation from the entry, finishing with, "How's that for sleuthing? Now all I have to do is get an invite to Nelson's office so I can check out that trophy."

"No, you don't. If Nelson thinks you're connected to Desota, who knows what he really wants from you. If the situation warrants, I'll go."

Like hell!

"I'll run Doyle and Kinsey by Donovan, the detective who investigated the fire," Ryan added. He paused for a second as they got into heavier traffic. "There's not much to eat at your sister's place. Are you hungry or did Nelson fill you up on dainty little tea sandwiches?"

She glared at him. "What is that supposed to mean?"

"I don't know," he growled.

"You're jealous. Of Nelson."

"I am not jealous."

"You sure are acting jealous," she said.

"Why would I be jealous?"

"Good question. Why?"

"There's a deli a block or two over."

"Knock yourself out," she said.

As he maneuvered the car through a busy intersection, she added, "There are also the two women, Irene and Madeline, to consider. Irene is suspicious of Nelson but I'm not sure if it's only because she thinks he's basically dishonest. Katie led Irene to believe she was interested in Nelson as marriage material and wanted to make sure he isn't a criminal. As for Nelson, he's obsessed with his stepmother's money. And judging from the way he acted when we were alone, Katie was leading him on to get to the truth."

"That does it," Ryan announced as he pulled into a parking lot next to a place called Sea Shanty Deli. "You have to stay away from Nelson Lingford. And that means his downtown office as well as his home. Better yet, stay away from all of them!"

There he went with more autocratic decisions. Before she could react, he had parked the car and stepped outside into the drizzle.

She ended up ordering him a sandwich and herself a double chocolate shake while he called Donovan, who wasn't in the office. "He'll call me back when he can," Ryan said as he carried their tray to a table by a window.

They ate in virtual silence, Tess still annoyed with Ryan's heavy-handed proclamations. Wait until he heard she'd accepted a job at the residence.

The drive back to Katie's place was over in a couple of minutes. As they rolled to a stop in front of the building, Ryan said, "While you were in Bluebird House this morning, I made arrangements with a friend of mine to fix Katie's door. He said he'd drop the new key in the mailbox. I'll come up with you—"

"No, thanks. Whoever came yesterday was looking for something. They tore the place apart. They either found it or decided it wasn't there, and now the door is fixed. End of story."

He stared at her a moment. "You're still angry with me for breaking in on you at the Lingford place."

There didn't seem to any point in denying it, so she said nothing.

"You have to remember that I'm a cop—"

"And I'm the one who is going to get to the bottom of this," she interrupted. "Thanks to Katie, I'm the one with the ticket in the front door, the one with the job helping Madeline Lingford organize photos of her paintings."

"You can't be serious."

She opened her door. "Watch me," she said, levering herself out of the car using her crutches just in case an interested party was looking. She bent and peered back inside the car. "If you still want to help me on this,

I'll be ready to leave tomorrow morning before nine."

The knot was back in his jaw.

"Goodbye, Ryan."

Using the much-hated crutches to maneuver inside the building, she got out Katie's keys and found the one that opened the mail box. Sure enough, a shiny new gold key lay in the bottom of the box along with three pieces of junk mail, which Tess left in place. Pocketing the old key ring, she rode the elevator to the second floor where once again the old grouch cast her a glowering look from his post outside his apartment.

He opened the door as she passed, and Tess paused. An elderly shepherd mix had poked his nose out.

"You have a dog," she said, surprised.

"Hmph—" the old man snarled.

The dog had shuffled partway into the hall, and Tess leaned down to pat his head. "What's wrong with his eye?"

"Nothin' that concerns you," the man snarled.

She gently turned the dog's head in her hand, investigating the weeping eye from different directions, finally seeing the point of a sticker extruding from the lower eyelid. "Does your dog have a veterinarian?"

"Waste of money," the man said. Tess looked from his threadbare sweater to the shabby furniture visible through the crack in the door and understood the defensive posturing. He saw her staring past him and hugged the door closer to his hip as though ashamed of his poverty. "I think your pooch has a sticker in his eye," she said. "Unusual for winter, but not unheard of. Maybe he was rooting around in some old weeds or something."

The man frowned. "Could be," he said.

"Okay. I need you to get me a few things. A clean cloth, a towel will do. Bottled water. Small tweezers, a flashlight, a little bowl. Bring them all out here. I'll wait out here with your dog."

He stared at her hard before finally nodding. She'd expected him to take his dog and slam the door in her face. As she leaned against the wall the old man's dog sat down next to her legs. He pawed at his eye a couple of times but stopped when she told him to and looked up at her. This was what Tess loved about animals, and as she gently stroked his head, she knew he was content in his doggy way, even though his eye was bothering him.

Eventually the old man came back juggling everything Tess had asked for. While he held the flashlight, she flushed the eye, using the bowl to catch the excess, then maneuvered the tweezers to gently extract the sticker. She flushed the eye again and patted it dry, rewarded with a gentle flick of the dog's tongue across her hand and a thumping of his tail on the floor.

"Good as new," Tess said, standing.

The man's arthritic fingers fumbled with his pet's floppy ears in a fond gesture both man and animal seemed to enjoy. He seemed to be at a loss for words.

"He'll be fine," she said, briefly touching the man's arm before once again fumbling with the crutches and hobbling toward Katie's apartment.

Two pet situations in one day. Life as she knew it, as she liked it. Real life. People needed their animals, especially people who lived alone, who had few friends. Sometimes their pets were their only family.

She paused at Katie's door, glancing back down the hall. The man and his dog were gone, and she smiled. The smile slid away when she found Ryan's buddy hadn't actually gotten around to fixing the front door. So why had he left a new key? She stuck it in her pocket with all the other keys, vastly annoyed.

Well, she wouldn't call Ryan. No way. Better to pile the furniture in front of the door than deal with Ryan right now. She pushed open the door with the tip of one crutch, flipped on the light and stood stock-still.

The place had been ransacked again!

Before she could even begin to process that bit of news, a bigger problem launched itself out from behind the door as a man dressed in dark clothes with a stocking over his face grabbed at her. She reacted without thinking, flinging the crutches at him as she turned, heading back into the hall. The man caught her coat and she struggled free of it, her purse slipping off with the coat. Even her unbuttoned sweater fell around her feet, almost tripping her as she stumbled down the hall, gasping for breath.

She had to reach the old man's door, but even as that thought entered her mind it was followed by another. What could he do? Her assailant caught her again, this time by the shoulder, ripping the dress, fingers digging into her skin, catching her so hard she flew back against his unyielding body.

She felt a small circle of cold steel press against her throat as he twisted her left arm in back of her. She prayed the lady with the Dalmatian would choose that moment to walk her dog.

"Say one word and you're dead," the man said. It wasn't until that moment it dawned on her she hadn't made a peep.

He forced her back down the hall and into Katie's apartment, walking behind her, her arm twisted between them. They stepped over her coat. Her purse had spilled its contents when it fell. One mud-encrusted black boot landed on it full force. The man stopped for a second and used that same foot to kick everything back inside. He shut the door with a softness that stunned her with its civility.

And yet his grip was as tight and merciless as ever. One more twist on her arm and it would snap. But he hadn't killed her outright; there might be a chance of survival.

He pushed her ahead of him into the bedroom. The door closed behind them as the bed loomed into sight and any hope the elderly man down the hall might hear a scuffle and call for help died. It was too late now.

Her knees touched the bed. A primal jab of horror shot through her core. She screamed Ryan's name without producing so much as a squeak.

The man pushed her past the bed and slammed her against the far wall so hard her nose made a funny noise and her eyes watered. He twisted her head to the side, crunching the big black glasses against her temple and the side of her nose until they sprang off her face and fell to the floor. A hard stone of fear settled in her stomach.

"Listen carefully," he said. "I ought to shoot you right now, but I'm not going to. Understand?"

He ran the gun muzzle up and down her throat as he spoke. She tried to take in details. Silver gun. Four- or five-inch muzzle, plastic gloves on his hand, the kind surgeons wear, the cloying smell of baby powder. The plaster wall grated into her cheek as she nodded.

"You've been sticking your nose into places where it doesn't belong," he said, the gun coming to a stop against her cheek.

Tess stopped struggling. She concentrated

on listening, but it was hard with blood pounding in her ears.

"Mind your own business. Go back to your own life while you still have one to go back to, understand?"

She nodded again.

His grip dug into her arm as he leaned even closer. "Where is it?" he said.

"I don't know what—"

He yanked upward on her arm as the gun ground into her cheekbone. Pain shot through her shoulder, blinding her for a moment with its sheer intensity. Tears burned her eyes. "Don't try that with me, Katie."

Tess jerked. *Katie!*

"Of course I know your name," the man spat. "You think your daddy didn't talk about you? He never mentioned how pretty you are, though."

Tess swallowed the knot in her throat.

"I want his share of the fire money," her attacker said. "Fifty thousand. It's not here, so where did you stash it?"

Fire money? There had to be a mistake, an explanation.

"Get this straight," he said, yanking on her arm yet again, pinning her tighter against the wall by leaning his weight into her back.

She could barely breathe. The gun rested on her shoulder. "That money is mine now. I did the work, I took the risks, you have no rights to it. I'll do whatever I need to do to get it. Do you understand?"

"I need time," she croaked, her mind racing.

"Time?"

"I need a few days," she said, putting everything on the line. "I gave it to someone to keep. I won't tell you who. Kill me right now and I won't tell you who."

Another yank on the arm with a hurried, "Don't tempt me." He apparently thought it over before adding, "You've got till four o'clock tomorrow afternoon. Four o'clock. One second more, and you'll wish I'd taken you up on your offer. You understand?"

Her cheek on fire, she nodded again.

"I know your cell phone number," he said as once again the gun nuzzle jabbed her throat. "I'll call you tomorrow at four with a drop spot. Try any tricks, I'll go straight for the widow lady. Or maybe you'd rather I plug that new boyfriend of yours or the nice old guy down the hall? And his dog. Either way, after I kill one of them or all of them, I'll come looking for you."

"I understand."

"And keep your nose out of other people's business or I may just blow it clean off you face."

He pulled her with him as he stepped away from the wall, pushed open the bathroom door and shoved her inside. Tess sprawled on the linoleum floor. For one instant she got a look at the man's face, features distorted under the nylon stocking, squashed and anonymous. He slammed the door. It was silent for a second, then she heard footsteps. She sprang to her feet and locked the door before flinging herself back against the wall and holding her breath.

RYAN FED HIS CAT before changing out of his damp clothes, then spent a few minutes checking his e-mail. After that he wandered around his apartment, restless and irritated. There'd been a message on his machine when he got home telling him his buddy had fixed Katie's lock so he knew Tess was safe, but the tension eating away at him wouldn't subside.

Tess had called him jealous, and, Lord help him, he thought she might be right. One look at Nelson Lingford groping her had driven every professional bone from his body.

Still, would it have killed her to thank him for rescuing her instead of getting all hot under the collar? The woman wasn't a real undercover cop, she was a veterinarian! Her play acting had gone to her head. And now she claimed she had actually accepted a job at the Lingford house.

Well, she couldn't go. He'd seen Lingford's face behind Tess. He'd seen the conniving glint in the man's eyes. And if he thought an enemy of his had sent her, who knew what he had planned.

But she would go and he knew it and if he didn't give her some space, she'd shut him out and do it alone.

Clive jumped up on top of the bookcase, knocking over a few dust catchers. Ryan absently picked a wooden carving off the floor and set a photograph straight.

"You're losing your touch," he told the cat who sat in a smug, neat bundle. "Maybe you should lay off the cat food."

The photograph caught Ryan's attention, and he picked it up again. Peter stood by his first new car, a red two-door, used and dented, a high school graduation gift from their distant grandparents who'd been bliss-fully unaware when he sold it the next day for easy cash. His brother looked proud and happy, a young man on the brink of a bright and promising future. In truth, he'd been anything but happy and less than a week away from dying.

Ryan put the photo down and met his cat's unblinking gaze.

He dug Tess's phone out of his pocket and suddenly the image of her scrolling through the photo gallery popped into his head. He pushed a few buttons on the phone, working his way through a dozen menus until he found the right one. He left his apartment as his printer ground out the first photo.

FIRST HE DROVE by Desota's business, an electrical contracting place he'd driven by a hundred times. He hadn't paid it much atten-tion lately and was surprised to see a closed sign on the door in the middle of the day. Calling dispatch, he got a home address for Desota and drove on over.

Desota lived in a nice little community east of town. His house was two stories, rel-atively new, one of those places that occupy most of the lot to cut down on yard work. A broken tricycle and a coiled hose lay in the driveway. A notice of repossession had been taped to the front door.

Desota wasn't living in the house anymore. He'd lost his business, and from what Tess said, his family had deserted him. Donovan had questioned Desota about the fire—it was in the reports Ryan had read before taking a leave of absence. Desota had come into a hunk of change near the time of the fire, but it had been traced back to a savings and loan outfit. In the end, the loan hadn't been enough to bail him out.

Vince Desota was beginning to sound like a man with little else to lose.

Ryan drove to Tess's place next. All his rehearsed apologies for acting like a jerk were forgotten when he found signs that Katie's apartment had been broken into again. Pulling his gun, he nudged the door open.

It had obviously been searched, though not as thoroughly as before. More alarming were Tess's crutches on the floor along with her coat, sweater, purse and its contents. Other than a little dried mud on the carpet, there was no sign of another person. He opened the coat closet, peered inside and left the door ajar.

The bedroom was next and he opened that door with caution, dreading what he would find. She'd obviously been attacked at the door, dragged into the bedroom, God knows what happened next. She was just inside, dead or hurt and he was too late...

His gaze went immediately to the bloody smear on the bedroom wall, then to the closed bathroom door.

His heart leaped. "Tess?" he yelled, knocking on the door with the butt of the gun while pulling on the knob. He was about ready to kick the door in when it flew open.

She stood as still as death, scarlet scrapes vivid against white skin, a fist of knuckles crammed against her teeth as though to keep herself from screaming. Her dress was torn, her bandages trailed down her cheek.

"What happened?" he said, stepping toward her, expecting her, *needing her*, to fly into his arms for comfort. Something in her expression nailed his shoes to the floor and he stayed where he was.

"Tess?"

She lowered her hand deliberately. "I...I had a...visitor," she mumbled, her voice raw. He felt a chill in his heart as she added, "A man."

"Honey—"

"A big man…with a stocking over his face," she added. "I don't know who…I couldn't tell who…I thought he had come back…I thought you were him."

"Did he hurt you? Are you hurt?"

She was so quiet it scared him, though intellectually he knew victims of violent crimes sometimes reacted in this detached way as though trying to control emotions too fragile to face.

Reholstering his gun, his calm voice at odds with the molten lava churning in his gut, he said, "What did he want?"

"He roughed me up, that's all," she said, darting a glance at her feet and the door, anywhere but at him.

He scanned her with a critical eye. Bruises on her neck, abrasions across her right cheek and forehead, the bridge of her nose swollen. She rolled her left shoulder.

"What do you mean he roughed you up?"

"Against the wall," she answered, her voice cracking as she continued. "He ran a big silver gun up and down my face. He told me to mind my own business. He twisted my arm, pushed me against the wall. I need…I want to take a shower. Will you stay here until I'm done?"

He stared at her hard. Rape victims often wanted hot, scalding showers to wash away the feel and scent of an attacker.

"Did he—"

"No," she said. "Ryan, you'll stay, won't you?"

"Of course I'll stay." He ached to hug her.

She nodded gravely as she whispered, "Thank you."

TESS DROPPED THE SOAP so many times she finally left it at her feet, atop the drain, turning her face into the spray and closing her eyes.

She wanted to go home.

She wasn't a spy. She wasn't brave like Katie. She wanted to be a million miles away when the call from that man came.

But Katie wasn't a million miles away. Sooner or later she'd wake up and have to face this unless Tess managed to face it for her.

The question remained: how much to tell Ryan. She didn't know how to assimilate what she'd heard today. She would need to run it by him, but she was loath to mention the money and yet how could she not when that thug had sworn to come after her again? Where was she supposed to come up with fifty thousand dollars? And if she didn't, what would he do to her or Madeline Lingford or the man with the dog…even the dog…in retaliation?

Or Ryan…

Had her father taken fifty thousand dollars to purposely try to kill a woman?

Wasn't that a lot of money for just starting a fire?

She needed time to think. If she told Ryan about the money, he'd leap to the obvious conclusion that her father had burned down that house with the intent to kill. It would be like handing him her father. She couldn't imagine Katie would want that.

Oh, Katie, wake up, wake up.

There had to be another explanation. Until she figured it out, she wouldn't tell Ryan about the money.

The key was stamped 119. She needed to find out what that key opened. How hard could that be? She'd visit a locksmith, start there. She had Katie's car, and if she relented a little on the pretense of having a broken leg, she could drive herself around. All she needed to do was ditch Ryan.

Since her duffel bag was still at the hospital in Katie's room, Tess dressed in more of her sister's clothes, this time jeans and a woolly white sweater. Her straight red hair jolted her every time she glanced in the mirror, and now the clothes looked strange, too, the jeans a style she wouldn't have chosen, lower cut, tighter, the sweater sliding off one shoulder. Katie's taste or Katie's disguise?

Whichever, the different look only emphasized Tess's increasing disassociation from her own life. She longed to speak to her mother, wherever she was. Barring her mother, a friend would do, but she hadn't recovered Katie's cell phone from Ryan and the thought of leaving the apartment to hunt for a pay phone made her shiver.

He was out there.

Besides, how could she explain what was happening to her? Her friends were normal people, people she worked with, had dinner with, went to movies with, laughed and plotted and shopped with. They had no more experience with violence than she did.

When she returned to the living room, she

found Ryan had straightened the place up again. He turned from where he stood at the sink and stared at her. No longer wet and bedraggled looking, he appeared trim and vigorous in tight blue jeans and a body-hugging navy T-shirt with a small police logo on the chest and long sleeves pushed up to his elbows. The muscles in his upper arms mesmerized her for a second. All that power, right there. What would he do if she ran to him? Would he hold her? Kiss her?

Wouldn't that be using him? Wouldn't that be unfair to him? And wouldn't that be giving in to the vulnerability that currently rocked her soul?

"You look better," he said, drying his hands on a striped dish towel. He leaned back against the counter, his arms folded across his chest, his gaze intense. At last he said, "Tess, I'm sorry. I should never have allowed you to come back here alone. I let my emotions—"

"Let's talk about what happened today," she said, cutting him off.

He reached out a hand, but she pretended she didn't see it and turned away. By omission, she was about to lie to him, and she hated herself for it.

Bypassing the love seat and the big recliner, she settled on a small chair. Ryan sat on the love seat by himself, leaning forward the way he did when listening, resting his forearms on his thighs, pinning her with his gaze. He looked as he had when she'd first met him: competent and strong. And she liked the fact that she could see a little of his gun. She almost wished the thug would come back. If Ryan shot him dead, the threat would be over.

Good heavens, what was happening to her?

"Tess?"

"He was in the apartment when I got here," she said.

"Hiding I assume."

"I was...preoccupied."

"You were mad at me."

"I should have realized something was wrong when I saw the busted lock. I mean, I was holding the new key your friend had made, so I knew he'd been here, and yet I didn't walk away. Why didn't I have the good sense to walk away?"

"Because you're new to this," he said softly. "Because you take things at face value."

She ignored the undercurrent of meaning

in his remark and continued. "He just came from out of nowhere. He grabbed me and took me into the bedroom. I thought he was going to—"

She stopped abruptly and swallowed. Her throat hurt. "He slammed me against the wall. He told me to mind my own business. He called me Katie."

Ryan jumped to his feet. "Katie! He called you Katie?" Pacing, he added, "If Nelson Lingford sent this thug, then your cover at that house is blown. You can't go back there. Wait, maybe the creep's lying to you. Maybe he found Katie's belongings in her closet."

"No, I checked, the stash is still there, all tucked away. He knew my name before he came here."

"Not your name, your sister's name."

"Sometimes it gets confusing. Sometimes I forget where she ends and I start."

His voice earnest, he said, "I know you're scared, but before we call the police in, you have to tell me everything that happened to you today."

"I'm trying to tell you," she said, tears burning behind her nose. "But you have to stop throwing out edicts. And don't forget this, Ryan—the police washed their hands of this matter. I don't want them involved, that's what you're here for. I'm just trying to find out who framed my father. I need you to help me, not bully me."

He ran a hand though his hair and stared at her. She saw his gaze dart to the bruises on her throat.

"We have to call the police," he said.

"You're the police."

"You know what I mean. Katie's accident could have been just that, an accident. The first ransacking of her apartment could have been the work of opportunistic thieves. This attack on you is different. There's no subtle way to interpret it."

"No. They'll use this to further condemn my father."

"Why would they do that?"

She'd said too much! As far as Ryan knew, the intruder had only warned her to stop snooping. He didn't know about the demand for money. Clasping her hands together, she said, "No police. We agreed. What happened today just shows that I'm getting close to someone."

Ryan closed his eyes for a second. She couldn't begin to guess what he was thinking. "Let's go to my apartment," he said at last, his eyes open again but troubled like a stormy winter sea.

"I want to stay here," she said at great cost. The thought of sleeping in this apartment after the terror of the afternoon sickened her. But she wouldn't leave.

Ryan nodded, accepting her decision though she could tell he hated it.

"And you won't call the police. There's nothing I can tell them about that man. He wore gloves and a mask."

"No police, not yet," he agreed ominously.

Tess got to her feet. "I want to see Katie."

"Are you sure you're up to—"

"I need to see her," Tess said, tears filling her eyes. "I need to see her breathe in and out. I need to make sure she's okay, that no one got to her...."

Ryan reached for her hand. "Let's go."

Chapter Seven

They stopped at the Lum Yuen restaurant for egg flower soup before they hit the hospital. Not that Tess made much headway on hers. Ryan couldn't help but notice the way she glanced at the door every time it opened and her startled response when a waiter dropped an empty tray. She was a bundle of raw nerves, looking over her shoulder, biting her lip, having a hard time making conversation.

He should have taken her out for dessert, not soup.

Ryan paid the bill, and they drove to the hospital where they found Katie in the same condition as the day before. While Tess went out in the hall to talk to the doctor, Ryan stared down at Katie. Her bruises had faded a little, and the scrapes were mending. In some ways she now looked better than Tess.

The sisters' resemblance to one another was unmistakable and yet he saw differences between them, as well. Tess had rounder cheeks, longer lashes, fuller lips. But Ryan also acknowledged a new swelling of concern for Katie that went beyond his guilt for her current predicament. He was beginning to feel true compassion for her losses, and respect for her decision to search for the answers she needed. Answers that apparently had landed her here in this bed.

Answers Ryan knew she would detest.

He found Tess out in the hall by the phones. Once again she'd tried to reach her mother and once again had ended up leaving a message.

"Give me the word and I'll make a few calls," he said, taking Tess's hand and leading her out of the hospital. She'd left the crutches in the car. It was an underground parking area, and he'd let Tess off by the elevator. It was taking a chance, they agreed, that whoever was behind the earlier attack hadn't followed them into the hospital. But Tess couldn't very well show up feigning injuries at the hospital. She wore a scarf over her red hair.

On the drive back to Katie's apartment,

Detective Donovan finally returned Ryan's call. Both Doyle and Kinsey had been cleared right after the fire. Donovan wanted to know why Ryan was looking into this angle of the affair when it had proved to be a dead end.

Ryan hemmed and hawed a bit, finally saying he was helping Matt Fields's other daughter come to grips with all that happened, and that included presenting her with enough information to make her understand the search for the truth had been careful and unbiased.

"Send her in to talk to me," Donovan said as Ryan had known he would.

Ryan promised he would tell her.

They resettled in Katie's apartment as Ryan once again led Tess through the day's events. Obviously angry with herself, at one point she said, "I broke character in front of both Lingfords." She sat prim and proper in the chair, knees together, hands folded in her lap. He was reminded of a witness on a stand.

"Madeline has a little dog I think has salmon poisoning," she continued. "I didn't know Nelson was watching as I conducted a modest examination and asked a few questions to make a diagnosis. But the dog was really sick and I just kind of lost my head."

He shrugged it off. He couldn't see that Nelson's impression of her ability with animals made the slightest difference to anything.

"And then I was offered the job of helping with the art."

"I don't get that," he said. "What art? I thought all but five or six paintings were destroyed in the fire."

"That's true. But Madeline seems determined to put together a photographic album of the paintings. I'll find out more tomorrow."

He kept quiet. She wasn't going back there but he wasn't going to reopen that can of worms tonight.

"After that, Nelson wanted to see me. He got all friendly. I asked about what he and Katie had talked about before her accident. You came, and then we went to lunch."

"Giving Nelson Lingford plenty of time to come here and try to scare you to death."

"Except there was no way my attacker was Nelson Lingford or Vince Desota, for that matter. He was taller than either of them, burlier, his voice deeper."

"So Nelson hired out the job of terrorizing you."

"Or maybe Nelson didn't have a thing to do with it. Vince Desota saw me at Nelson's house. For all we know, Katie talked to him, too. Maybe he sent someone to threaten her. Me. Or maybe Irene did or Madeline or Muffy for heaven's sake!"

A brief smile was followed by, "Did the creep say anything that connected him to anyone else?"

"No," she said after an imperceptible pause. "But he acted like he was used to terrorizing people."

"Two-bit thugs always sound the same," he said. "They watch way too much television."

She nodded, but he noticed her eyes didn't meet his. He had the sudden suspicion she wasn't leveling with him.

"Anything else?" he asked.

She met his gaze then dropped hers and shook her head. "I'm exhausted," she said.

He studied her for a moment, sure she was being evasive, but unable to force himself to push her. Her eye was black now for real, probably from where the bridge of the glasses had been shoved into her face. The abrasions and bruises on her cheek gave her role as an accident victim a validity it had lacked that morning. She looked battered and tired, and once again he recalled the lovely blond vet who had bravely stepped into her twin sister's hospital room and subsequently into his life.

The past few days had been hard on her. She wasn't even demanding pancakes and hamburgers anymore.

"We'll go to bed then," he said.

She nodded once and got up. In a few minutes she brought him a pillow and a blanket, and then she stopped before walking away, came back and touched his arm. "Thank you," she said.

He wanted to pull her into his arms. His hands tingled with the desire to comfort her and maybe himself. Before he could make that mistake, she was gone, closing the bedroom door behind her, and he was left to make a bed in the old recliner and try not to think too hard about Theresa Mays.

TESS LAY AWAKE listening to her conscience.

How could she not have told Ryan the full extent of what that thug had wanted? She had to tell him. She couldn't face that man again without the money and she didn't know how to find the money.

On the other hand, Ryan knew there was

an extra key on Katie's key ring. Didn't the fact that he hadn't done anything with it mean he didn't know *what* to do with it?

He doesn't know about the money. He assumes, like you did, that the key opens the storage locker in which Katie stashed all her belongings. If he knew there was missing money he'd have a reason to give the spare key an extra look.

But what about Katie? If she'd hidden the money in a storage locker, then she knew their father had been involved in something illegal. Would Katie be pushing an investigation of her own if she knew their father was guilty? Of course not! That meant the extra key opened something totally innocuous and that when Mr. Thug returned, Tess would have nothing to offer him.

She needed help.

Katie was in the hospital. Tess was all banged up. She needed Ryan.

The clock in her head, the one steadily ticking away the hours, propelled her out of bed. She needed Ryan because he was a pro and she was an animal doctor. Nothing personal.

What about Katie? What about your father's innocence?

No matter. She had to tell Ryan.

She opened the bedroom door to find him asleep on the recliner, his head all askew. She approached quietly, looking at his face in the soft light coming through the sheer drapes, more shadows than not, but she was getting used to him now, she could fill in the blanks for herself.

He seemed restless as though caught in some kind of dream. He'd slept the same way the night before, and she wondered what tortured him when he slept, what haunted him when his defenses were down.

What would he do if she kissed his brow and whispered his name?

SOMETHING WOKE RYAN. An air current, an odor, a noise. Something alerted him, something clued his brain that despite all precautions, Tess's attacker had found a way back inside the apartment. He grabbed upward, connecting with a wrist, pulling and diving at the same time. Thrust from sleep, adrenaline kicking into high gear, he didn't take time to think, just to act. He and his assailant flew to the carpet where Ryan pinned the other man under him.

Breathing heavily, it took him a second to

pick up a subtle female scent. In that instant the threads flung across his arm became silky strands of hair while the body crushed beneath his shrank to the size and shape of a woman.

Tess.

He immediately rolled off her, muttering, "I'm sorry." Embarrassment kept him flat on his back, staring straight up at the ceiling.

"It's okay," she gasped, her soft voice arousing a dozen conflicting feelings in his gut. He turned his head to look at her and found she'd rolled onto her side and now regarded him with her head propped on her hand.

"You have quick reactions," she said breathlessly.

His short laugh was full of irony as he said, "Oh, yeah. I'm deadly when it comes to beautiful lady veterinarians."

"You thought I was someone else."

Soft light coming through the windows sparkled on her hair, glittered in the whites of her eyes and the flash of her teeth as she spoke. The rest of her body formed dark curves against the beige carpet. He fought a strong desire to roll back on top of her.

"What do you dream about?" she asked.

The question startled him.

"Something troubles you," she persisted.

"*You* trouble me," he murmured.

"Something else," she insisted. "I've watched you sleep."

He'd never talked to anyone about Peter. Not his parents, nor to the police, because his actions or lack thereof had nothing to do with the investigation of Peter's sordid death. No one. He'd swallowed his guilt and kept it inside, taking on an immediate assignment to help track down the drug connections that had helped kill his brother, finding no solace when it was over. He'd assumed that after a few weeks, a few months, the feelings of shame and remorse would fade away.

And, truthfully, it seemed as though that's just what had happened until Matt Fields's lies had scorched not only his own disintegrating life but the lives of those around him.

Now Ryan found himself back at square one.

"You have nightmares," she persisted.

"No."

"Oh, Ryan. Something troubles you so much you can't escape it when you sleep. Why won't you talk to me?"

"Because it has nothing to do with you," he said. "Because there's no way to fix it, no reason to get into it. Why did you come out here, anyway? Did you hear something?"

She stared at him.

"What aren't you telling me?" he demanded, propping himself up a bit more so he could look down at her.

"Nothing. I—"

"Come clean," he said. "I've known all night that something happened today you're keeping to yourself. How am I supposed to help you, how am I supposed to keep you safe if you don't trust me?"

"I do trust you," she protested.

"No, Tess, you don't."

"I do—"

"Then what happened? Did that thug molest you?"

She was silent. Had he hit the nail on the head? A sick feeling filled his gut.

He reached over and gently stroked her cheek, her skin so soft beneath his fingers...

"He hurt me and he scared me but he didn't molest me," she said.

"I'm so sorry I wasn't here for you," Ryan said, reaching up to fondle the fine tresses of her hair. He expected her to grab his hand

and stop him as his fingers drifted to her cheek and down her lovely chin.

"I'm glad you weren't here," she said.

"Hmm—"

"He probably figured he could intimidate and control me. No doubt he would have shot you right away."

"You're not making me feel any better about this," he told her with a wry smile.

"I don't want you hurt," she whispered.

"I don't want you hurt, either," he said. "Your bravery terrifies me."

"My bravery? I'm trembling inside."

"So am I," he said and he could tell by the fluttering of her lashes she realized he wasn't talking about fear. Her fluttering lashes mimicked the sudden quiver of his heart. He ached for her in a way he hadn't ached for a woman in too long to remember. He waited for the slightest indication that she wanted him to stop caressing her.

Instead she placed her free hand around his neck, rolled onto her back and pulled him so close their lips touched. Desire leaped through his body like an uncaged beast.

"There's something between us," she whispered.

"Just a few thin articles of clothing," he said, toying with the neckline of her gown.

He sensed her smile. "I mean something physical."

"I know."

"But that's all it is," she added, a note of urgency in her voice.

Like hell, he thought, but kept it to himself.

She swallowed as he ran his fingers down her throat. Before he could lecture himself on the inadvisability of becoming sexually involved with a woman he'd sworn to protect, her open mouth met his, hot and wet, softer than velvet, her tongue sliding against his, the roar in his head obliterating the last spark of good sense.

She ran her fingers through his hair, her grasp on his neck stronger as they kissed again and again, deep kisses that surfaced quickly, exploratory at first evolving to rabid in the blink of an eye. He trailed kisses down her chest, nestling his head in the valley between her cotton-covered breasts, his fingers flicking over her gown, her nipples becoming pebbles beneath the fine fabric, his mouth following his touch.

She moaned, and the next thing he knew

she was pulling on his clothes. He got to his feet, pulling her up after him. It took him a second to take off the gun and lay it aside, to strip bare. She didn't follow suit, just stood there in her short gown. He'd never had a woman watch him undress before. Her attention was exciting, the gentle smile curving her lips, enticing.

He went to her and pulled her gown over her head, revealing her supple body, his to touch and admire, to devour. She fairly sparkled in the heavily shadowed light, small but round, fragile but vital, a dozen radiant shades of silver. He cupped her face and kissed her with the intention of carrying her off to bed at the first opportunity, but she pulled down on his shoulders and together they sank to their knees, their arms entwined, their mouths connected until they hit the carpet. She pushed him down on his back, gently, softly, and then she climbed astride him, her hips over his, his arousal hard between them.

The outside light illuminated the planes of her face, the mounds of her breasts and the soft curve of her belly as she spread her fingers across his chest and leaned over his face, her hair cascading forward, spilling onto his shoulders. Her mouth was moist, stoked by the same fire as his. He reached around her waist and slid his hands down to cup her bottom as she raised her head, her eyes closed. His fingers slid around to find her moist contours until she cried out with pleasure and, leaning forward again, kissed him deeply. Clasping her body close to his, he rolled her onto her back and plunged deep inside her. Release came quickly the first time, slower the next.

Eventually Tess fell asleep in his arms, her body tucked against his—a perfect fit, a natural duet, warmer and softer than anything else in the world.

But Ryan couldn't sleep. He stared into the dark, his gun within easy reach, waiting for the sound of footsteps in the hall. One thought refused to be quieted: had Tess made love to him because she'd been swept away by the same powerful emotions that had overcome him? Or had she made love to avoid confessing whatever had brought her into the room in the first place?

TESS AWOKE WITH A START, but knew at once exactly where she was and what had happened to bring her there. For a second she regarded the heavy arm draped over her shoulder. A warmth spread through her body like embers stirred with a poker.

Ryan cried out softly, his head buried against the back of her head, his voice muffled. He was in the midst of a dream; it was his apparent distress that had startled her awake.

She revolved in the circle of his arms to face him. His eyes moved behind his lids, darting this way and that as though trying to find something or someone. His brow furrowed, his lips twitched. "Peter," he whispered in such a heartbreaking voice that her breath caught.

She placed her lips on his and kissed him gently.

His eyes opened, the gray irises stormy, calming almost at once upon seeing her.

She kissed him again. "'Morning."

He blinked. The morning had dawned clear for once. Winter sunlight danced through the window, bathing his face with light. Squinting he said, "'Morning."

She said, "Who's Peter?"

It was as though a door closed behind his eyes. "My brother," he said at last.

"Tell me about him."

"He's dead, Tess."

"How—"

"Doesn't matter, does it? He's gone."

"Of course it matters. I don't know anything about you."

"I have two living sisters named Lisa and Heather, my parents, Connie and Donald, two aunts, three cousins, four uncles including Uncle Marty, who's serving ten years for embezzling his company's payroll, and six nephews. No nieces. Just nephews. If you and I are going to get married and have children, then we're going to have to produce at least one girl. If that doesn't sound doable to you, then tell me now so I can figure out how to break the news to Mom."

She smoothed a few strands of dark hair away from his brow, ignoring the jolt his words induced in her chest. "Stop joking. How did Peter die?"

He swallowed hard and said, "A drug overdose. When he was eighteen."

"I'm sorry."

He nodded.

She wanted to ask him why he blamed himself for his brother's drug overdose, but made herself be silent. He'd tell her when he was ready. Instead she said, "You and Katie never, ah, kissed…or anything…did you?"

"Absolutely not," he said.

"There were no feelings, no unrequited love—"

"Kind of late to be worrying about this, isn't it?"

"I got the feeling you barely knew her."

"Tess, stop worrying. I told you before. I never made a pass at Katie, and she never looked twice at me. Now it's your turn to answer a question. Tell me what you came in here to tell me last night. It has something to do with your attacker, doesn't it? You're keeping something back, something you know I should know."

Grabbing the blanket to her chest, she sat up and stared down at him. "How did you guess?"

"I'm a cop and I happen to be getting to know you. Plus, no offense, you're a terrible liar."

She nodded because she knew that was true. With a deep breath, the words tumbled out. "The man wanted the money he said my father was paid before the fire. Fifty thousand dollars, he said."

Ryan whistled as he sat up beside her.

"He said I had until this afternoon to come up with the money or what happened to Madeline Lingford or the old guy down the hall would be on my head, not my father's. And he threatened you. He told me he'd call me at four o'clock today. I need to get Katie's cell phone from you, Ryan."

"You gave him Katie's cell phone number?"

"Of course not. He said he knew it."

Ryan chewed on his lip. "I wonder how he got her number. Her phone's in with my stuff, I'll get it for you in a moment. Okay, what did you tell the creep?"

"I told him I had hidden the money with someone else and I wouldn't tell him who even if he killed me. He didn't seem surprised by this, so I assume the money is cash. If there is money. He might have been, oh, I don't know, bluffing, right? He might have been mistaken...."

"Of course it's cash," Ryan said, obviously thinking to himself. "We need to figure out what that extra key on Katie's ring opens."

"I thought of that, too. Like you said, with that 119 stamped on it, it must open a storage locker. Maybe she stored the money in with all her things. Ryan, I was thinking...are you sure those two names Irene Woodall gave me are useless? I mean, obviously Katie thought they were worth looking into, so perhaps she found out something about them that the police missed. Who are those men?"

He seemed to come back from someplace faraway, though he responded as though he'd registered every word she said. "Clint Doyle was Nelson Lingford's bodyguard at one time. He was fired a few days before the fire, and at first Donovan thought he might be carrying a grudge, but that didn't pan out. He wasn't employed at the time of the fire, but he and Kinsey went out drinking that night so they provided alibis for each other. Jim Kinsey was the widow's driver. Lingford let him go after the fire."

"She seems to be a virtual prisoner at his house," Tess said.

"At any rate, Donovan looked into Kinsey, too. But you have to remember the fire happened before Kinsey lost his job so what's the motive?

"Isn't money always a motive?" Tess asked.

He flashed her a grin. "Good point. Well, okay, remember Doyle gave him an alibi."

"Still, I think Katie must have suspected something. Maybe one of them framed our father—"

He touched her arm. "Whoa, Tess. What do you mean, 'framed' your father? The man took fifty thousand dollars. If that's not guilt—"

"Some two-bit thug *said* he took fifty thousand dollars," she corrected. "We have no idea if it's the truth."

"If you truly believe he's innocent, why didn't you tell me what the thug wanted right from the start? Why are you wondering if the extra key opens a locker where Katie stashed the money? If your father was framed, there is no money. Part of you must know your dad was guilty."

"I knew you'd take it like this," she said.

"Like what? Like reality?"

Gritting her teeth, she said, "Has it occurred to you that my father may have been working undercover?"

"Undercover? Without the knowledge of anyone at the department? Do you have any idea of the protocol—"

"Okay, maybe he took the money because someone was blackmailing him or threatening Katie. There could be lots of reasons. Katie knew him. She believed in him."

He stared at her a long moment before saying, "There's a bottom line here. Someone has ransacked your sister's apartment not once but twice looking for something. That someone took a chance by waiting for you and threatening you point-blank. I think it's safe to assume there is actual money lying around somewhere, that Katie knew about it, that someone with very little to lose wants it and is willing to harm you or Madeline Lingford to get it."

"Or you."

"And that probably means he hasn't made me as a cop, so there's the good news. Anyway, we need to find the money and use it to catch him."

"Can't we just pretend to have it?"

"If I thought this whole thing began or ended with your thug, yeah, sure, I guess we could try that. But it goes farther than him. We can use the money as a bargaining chip. If he wants it bad enough and I scare him badly enough, he might lead us to the real brains behind all this. I just want you to be prepared for the information that this will prove your father is guilty once and for all."

"I know," she said, trying her best not to

let him see how much she dreaded that possibility.

"Okay. Good. And there's another bottom line, as well. Whoever ran over Katie didn't do it to get at your father's money. They did it to shut her up. As far as they know, they failed because here you are walking around pretending to be her. This has the feel of two different agendas. Keep that in mind."

"I still have to go to Madeline's house this morning to help her with the art photos," she said, preparing herself for another argument. She didn't care what he said, she was going to keep that appointment.

"What about Nelson?"

"I'll be fine. I'm just going to look at a bunch of pictures. What about the guy down the hall and Madeline Lingford? The creep who attacked me threatened them, too."

"Why the guy down the hall? I understand Madeline Lingford, but him?"

"I can only think our thug witnessed me helping the old guy's dog. He might have decided the man is important to me. Truth is, he's right. I won't be responsible for anyone else being hurt—"

"They'll all be safe until after four o'clock. While you're shuffling through photos, I'll go question the bodyguard and the driver. And if I have time I'll see what Desota is up to, though I can't quite figure out why Desota would attack you unless he was in cahoots with your father to burn down the Lingford house."

"Or in cahoots with Nelson to frame my dad."

He suppressed a weary smile. She was nothing if not optimistic!

"I'm just glad you're going to look into Doyle's and Kinsey's alibis again."

"I never looked into them in the first place," he reminded her. "Donovan did. He's a thorough detective, but sometimes things shake loose after a certain amount of time has passed. It would be interesting, for instance, to see if either Doyle or Kinsey are living a little higher on the hog than they were two months ago. Maybe one of them had a sudden influx of fifty thousand bucks." He leaned forward and kissed her nose. "But I'll come pick you up by noon and we'll go looking for the locker. And be careful. If Nelson comes home and tries to get you off alone—"

"I'll be careful," she said.

He sprang to his feet effortlessly, and she

watched him walk across the floor, pull on his underwear—she'd been right, he did wear briefs—then retrieve Katie's phone.

Sexy guy.

She knew she shouldn't allow herself so much as a follow-up kiss to the previous night's folly, but she wasn't the love-'em-and-leave-'em type. He didn't seem the type, either. That's what bothered her. What they had started needed to end here. She had no intention of ever becoming dependent on a man.

Even a man like Ryan. Her mother's example had been quite convincing on that account.

But that didn't stop her body from responding to his. The images from the night before were vivid....

"Are you okay?" he said, halting in front of her.

Looking up, she licked her lips. "Fine? And you?"

He sank back down to the floor, peeling the blanket away, the heat in his hands reflecting the intensity of his eyes. "I'll let you know," he whispered as his lips traveled across her shoulder blade and down the slope of her breast to her belly. "You'll be the first to know."

Tess closed her eyes. Later. She'd think later. For now she would trust her feelings one last time.

Chapter Eight

Though Tess had taken only one art-appreciation class during her undergraduate days at college, she knew fine art when she saw it. The Lingford collection seemed to have focused on Impressionists like Matisse, Renoir and Cezanne, though a few paintings and their artists were more obscure.

"I'm stunned by the scope of this collection," Tess said as Madeline Lingford arranged eight-by-ten photographs of the destroyed paintings using the artists' names to reference them. There must have been more than two dozen paintings with several different shots taken of each. It was amazing how light and distance affected the presentation of the art. Each print was protected by a clear plastic cover. They were spread out across a long table set up in the music room.

Nelson himself had not made an appearance, though this didn't surprise Tess as Ryan had pinpointed Nelson's whereabouts before dropping her at the Lingford house. Tess thought Ryan's caution a little over the top; in this big house full of servants and with these two older women, she was no doubt safer than she'd been in days. Her main gripe was being cut off from Ryan and the "action."

Madeline brought her back to reality with a small sigh. "Weren't all my paintings pretty?" she said. "I think I liked the little dog running in the poppies the best. It reminded me of my Muffy."

"It was done by a local artist," Irene said gently. "Why not commission him to paint Muffy for real?"

"I could do that?"

"I'll contact him for you and arrange it," Irene said. She laughed and added, "Leave it to you to prefer a painting of a dog to a genuine Monet."

Madeline smiled. "I just know what I like."

Irene had been at the house when Tess arrived, either unwilling to leave Tess alone or to hand over her part of Madeline's project. It made Tess's presence rather unnecessary. Should she leave and pop up unannounced at Nelson's downtown office? She ached to see that trophy, to try to figure out why Katie had photographed it. Or should she stay where she was?

"Do you still travel to acquire art?" Tess asked Irene as she accepted her present situation.

"Not for me, she doesn't," Madeline said quickly. "I stopped buying art after Theo passed away."

"I have other clients," Irene said. "And I do love to travel on my client's dime!"

"Not me. I like my own house. But of course I don't have my own house anymore, and Nelson seems to think it's a waste for me to buy another."

"You should do what pleases *you*," Irene said.

"Yes, but, well, you see Nelson is the only family I have left. I'd never hurt his feelings. He installed that elevator and bought me a piano and he truly adores Muffy."

Tess jumped in with another question. "How is Muffy doing? Did she have salmon poisoning?"

"Your guess was right on the money,"

Madeline gushed. "Muffy's doctor says she'll make a full recovery. I'm expecting a call from him at any moment to tell me when I can bring her home."

Tess took a deep breath, trying not to look too satisfied with herself but missing her real life with a dull ache. That thought brought the inevitable follow-up thought. Real life meant saying goodbye to Ryan. He belonged to New Harbor, and her feelings for him were too intense to last, even if she wanted romance in her life.

And she didn't.

She blotted out thoughts of Ryan. Another, darker thought crossed her mind. If Nelson resented Muffy saving his stepmother and he had now poisoned the dog—salmon poisoning was always fatal if not treated—then did he have another plan in mind for getting rid of Madeline? She bit her lip as she thought. Weren't there a half-dozen paintings that had survived the fire? These were very valuable paintings. The insurance money from even one or two of them would be astronomical. Or wait. They hadn't been donated yet. If Madeline predeceased the donation, would Nelson inherit the paintings? Was getting rid of Muffy a first step?

"Where did you keep the art collection?" she asked.

"On the walls, of course," Madeline said, handing over a stack of photos of a stunning Degas. "My late husband insisted most of it be vaulted, but I got it all out after he died and had it hung on every wall in the house. Nelson said it was dangerous because of thieves. The cost of insurance meant the collection was underinsured, but I never had a break-in. It was a big old dark house, and the paintings brightened things up a lot."

"Wallpaper is meant to brighten things," Irene said softly. "Great art is meant to provoke."

"Hoity-toity words, Irene dear. You know I'm not a snob." She took off a pair of glasses almost as big as the ones Tess wore as part of her disguise and added, "I loved looking at those paintings. Every single day I visited every single one, and now there are only half a dozen left and most of those are damaged." She clasped Irene's hand and added, "I've been in constant contact with the people who reclaim fire-damaged art. They assure me that when all is said and done, at least four of them will survive, isn't that right, Irene?"

"I've talked to them, as well. It's a small number…"

"At least Theo's favorite, that wonderful Renoir, was saved. But, oh, this Monet. Gone forever. What a horrible pity." She handed a photo to Tess who admired the artist's use of light before Irene took it from her and placed it with the other Monets.

"How is it you have all these wonderful photos?" Tess asked.

Madeline beamed. "Irene and Georges took all the photographs. Aren't they splendid? I wanted a complete record before the collection was moved to the museum to be assessed. Georges is a fabulous photographer. You're so lucky to have him as an assistant, Irene."

"Don't I know it," Irene said.

"But I haven't seen him since soon after the fire."

"He's been so busy on special projects I've had to hire additional help. He's such a hard worker."

"And that's why you should be at your store and not here," Madeline said firmly. She looked up from a stack of photos. "A few photographs seem to be missing."

"I must have left a box upstairs," Irene said.

Tess tried a new question. "I gather Nelson wasn't too fond of the idea of donating the art to the museum."

Madeline smiled. "That, my dear, is an understatement! He tried to talk me out of it. He couldn't get past the millions it would be worth at auction."

"Speaking of Nelson, when do you expect him home?" Irene asked.

"Oh, not until late this afternoon. Meetings, you know. Nelson is almost as clever as his father was."

Tess's gaze met Irene's knowing eyes and slid away. She asked a question she knew the answer to. "Was Nelson with you the night of the fire?"

"No. He was supposed to be, but at the last moment he went to a concert. I was supposed to be at a charity function that night, but I didn't feel well so I went to bed. Muffy woke me when smoke filled the house, and I rang for the police. I barely got out alive. Would you believe a policeman was responsible for the fire? Isn't that reprehensible? Why would a man of the law do something like that?" She looked about ready to cry.

"I don't know," Tess whispered. Was it possible Madeline had never considered the possibility her stepson did it for the money? She was spared further comment when the maid appeared in the doorway. "The mail has come, Mrs. Lingford. I left it on Mr. Lingford's desk. And the veterinarian's office called. Muffy can come home. Shall I send the driver to fetch her?"

Madeline wheeled around in her chair, her dexterity amazing to Tess who hadn't seen her move herself since meeting her the day before. Those withered shoulders obviously held muscle. The good news about Muffy seemed to chase away the doldrums Tess's questions had created.

"Of course, of course, only I'm going, too!" she said. "Tell the driver to bring around the van with the hydraulic lift for my wheelchair." She looked back at Tess and added, "Nelson fired my driver. His driver isn't as good as my old one but he gets me around, and I just have to be there for Muffy. You understand, don't you, dear?"

"Absolutely," Tess said. "Why did Nelson fire your driver?"

"He had his own driver and decided it would be better after I moved out here if we combined our staffs and cut down on the overhead. I brought Ester and my chef."

"It's almost ten-thirty," Irene said. "Caroline and I can keep working for an hour at least. We'll probably still be here when you get back."

Madeline waved a hand as the woman who had answered the door the day before wheeled her out of the room. Tess handed Irene a stack of protected photos and said, "How is Tabitha, or do you see her every day?"

"Every single day," Irene said, "unless I'm traveling and then I call. I go over for breakfast most mornings unless she's too ill to eat, and then I sit by her bed and read her stories, just like I did when she was tiny."

Tess, who had fond memories of her own mother reading stories to her, smiled.

"I don't know how long Tabitha and I will have together," Irene said, her voice soft. "I'm just so grateful her father provided for her after his death so she can be comfortable and well looked after. Sometimes she's so sick it startles me and I don't think she can hold on, but so far she rallies."

"She looked healthy yesterday," Tess said.

"She loved visiting with you, by the way. Can't stop chattering about the kitty necklace. Now, let's talk about something a little less upsetting than Tabitha's future. How about those names I got for you yesterday? You asked for employees dismissed right around the time of the fire. Those were the only two." She spread a new assortment of photos on the table and began scribbling notes to herself.

"Why did Nelson have a bodyguard?"

Irene looked up from her notes. "I gather he had some unwanted attention from an old girlfriend, so for a time he employed a bodyguard." She made additional notes and handed Tess the photos to file, her gaze lingering on Tess's face. "You seem to be much better today, though your bruises look worse than ever," she said. "Some of those scrapes actually look new."

"Bruises often look worse as they heal," Tess said vaguely. "Excuse me for being blunt, Irene, but you don't like Nelson much, do you?"

Irene glanced toward the doorway again, then back at Tess. Lowering her voice, she said, "I know you think he's wonderful. I understand he could have that effect. But I don't like the way he thinks he's better than everyone else. His father wasn't like that and he was twice the man Nelson is or ever will be. Besides, I've seen Nelson associating with some very iffy business partners, if you know what I mean. I wouldn't put anything past him."

The first few notes of Beethoven's "Für Elise" broke the uneasy silence. Irene glanced at Tess's purse. "Isn't that your phone?"

Tess had never heard it ring. She dug it out of her bag, terrified her attacker was calling earlier than planned. The Caller ID didn't help because she didn't know anyone's number here. It did seem to be local so that ruled out her mother.

"Aren't you going to answer it?" Irene asked.

Tess stared at it a moment longer, scared to press a button, afraid she'd hear her attacker's low, guttural voice, afraid she'd throw up if she did. At last she relented and, holding her breath, clicked on the phone.

"Hey," Ryan said.

Gripping the corner of the table to keep from sagging from relief, she said, "Hi."

"I spent the last hour bar hopping, no easy feat this early in the morning. There's something fishy about the Kinsey/Doyle alibi."

"That's encouraging, right?"

"Could be. I'm on my way to see Doyle now."

"I should be with you," Tess said.

"You stay where you are, nice and safe."

It was on the tip of her tongue to protest this comment despite how precisely it reflected how she felt. She wanted to ask about Vince Desota but couldn't think of how to do it with Irene standing nearby. Instead she said, "What about the...um, key?"

"You have the key, remember? You also look just like your sister plus you hold her identification, so we'll do that together when I pick you up."

"I see. Well, it sounds like you've been lucky."

"I started my day lucky," he said with enough tease in his voice to make Tess smile shyly at the memory.

How could she leave him?

How could she stay?

She clicked off the phone, dropped it in her bag and met Irene's gaze.

"Is everything okay?"

"My cousin locked himself out of his car," she said. "He has an extra key so it's no big deal."

Irene nodded. She looked preoccupied

with the photos. "I'm going upstairs to hunt for that box of missing pictures," she said.

"I'll just go use the bathroom," Tess said, laying her purse aside.

If Irene was busy upstairs and Nelson and Madeline were away from the house, what better time to take a look in that big desk in Nelson's den?

CLINT DOYLE HAD LANDED on his size twelve-and-a-half feet by taking a job as a bodyguard for New Harbor's most famous female impersonator, a guy by the name of Marcel. Ryan had never actually been inside his club, as a good set of bouncers tended to keep this club—like the local strip joints— relatively crime free.

Ryan found Doyle right inside the door of Marcel's which, on this late Friday morning, was empty of patrons and bouncers. A full dress rehearsal was underway, however, complete with music.

Doyle himself was a redwood tree of a man, almost as broad as he was tall, hard as a rock, head shaved clean, facial features accented with a nose about the size and hue of a red potato. He wore a black T-shirt tucked into black jeans, a black jacket stretched tight over his shoulders, the bulge of a shoulder holster obvious.

Ryan had spent the morning hunting down and talking to a half-dozen bartenders who had corroborated the Kinsey/Doyle alibi, and gradually he'd developed a funny feeling about it all. The idea was beginning to float around in the back of Ryan's mind that Doyle and Kinsey were in cahoots. Maybe Kinsey was the torch and maybe he drove the car that almost killed Katie while Doyle searched her apartment. Maybe Doyle was trying to double-cross Kinsey by finding Tess's father's stash without telling Kinsey.

"I ain't leaving this spot," Doyle said, his gaze glued to the stage where Marcel himself, dressed in enough glitter and rhinestones to adorn a whole Las Vegas act, belted out a medley of Broadway tunes. Three other men sporting cleavage, curls and heels backed him up, but there was no mistaking the true star and that was Marcel. Well over six feet tall and wearing a dozen shades of purple feathers, his hair was styled in a pinkish beehive. He strutted and sang and looked more feminine, and thus less feminine, than any woman Ryan had ever seen.

"Marcel pays me damn good money to

watch his back, and that's what I'm going to do," Doyle added. "Lots of freaks in this town just waiting to get at him, but they won't, not when Clint Doyle is on the clock. Ask me whatever you want, detective, but I ain't leaving this spot."

Ryan leaned against the wall. He hadn't told Doyle he was a cop, the man just knew. "Let's start with where you were yesterday afternoon between two and three o'clock," Ryan said.

"Easy. Here."

"Anyone see you?"

Doyle gestured with his arm. "Everyone."

Ryan watched the three backup singers cavort around Marcel for a moment as his mind whirled. This club was two blocks up and six over from Katie's apartment. Doyle could easily have left here, driven there, torn the place apart, attacked Tess and been back by this door in less than thirty minutes. Dressed in black, standing in shadows, would anyone notice if he left for a few minutes?

"Did you talk to anyone?" he asked.

Doyle appeared to be thinking. He finally said, "Trista. Paulie."

"Who are Trista and Paulie?"

With a flip of his wrist and an extended thumb, Doyle gestured at the bar, which ran along the side of the club. "That's Trista. Paulie ain't in yet."

A young girl stood behind the bar, her gaze darting between the stage and Doyle, polishing and repolishing the same glass with a white cloth.

"I'll be back," Ryan told Doyle, and moseyed over to the bar. Trista, dark hair in pigtails, perky breasts poking at her red Marcel's T-shirt, looked at him as he approached. Was she old enough to be working in a nightclub?

"We're not open," she said, but the voice was wrong, it was too low, and then Ryan noticed a dark shadow on the clean-shaven jaw. He gave himself a mental slap for slowness and said, "I just want information. Did you talk to Clint Doyle yesterday?"

The boy behind the bar might look seventeen from a distance, but up close, at least to Ryan, there was a world-weary glint to his eye that pushed his age up a decade. "Sure. I took him iced tea and a sandwich. We ate our lunch together. Then Paulie came by and the two of them stood there for a long time, watching Marcel flit around the stage.

Wouldn't you think Clint would get tired of watching Marcel? I sure do."

"What time did you take him the sandwich?"

"I don't know, somewhere around two. He and Paulie stood over there a good hour after that."

Ryan wandered back to Doyle. The alibi for yesterday sounded pretty airtight but he doubted the D.A. or anyone else downtown would be impressed with the testimony of a cross-dressing bartender and someone named Paulie who spent his afternoons hanging around a nightclub. Ryan wasn't sure he was. Still, for this moment, he would accept Clint Doyle's alibi for the afternoon someone attacked Tess. And since Doyle didn't strike him as the most shrewd man in the room, just the most loyal, he thought of another tack he could try.

"How old is Trista?" he asked as he stood next to Doyle.

"Hell, I don't know."

"He doesn't look twenty-one."

"Ain't none of my business."

"I might make it your business," Ryan said casually. "Seems if Marcel got it in his head you ratted out an underage employee to the

Oregon Liquor Control Commission, he might stop signing those plump paychecks you currently enjoy."

For the first time, Doyle's gaze left the stage and fastened on Ryan. "Why don't you stop tiptoeing around and just tell me what you want."

"I want to know about your alibi for December first of last year. The night the Lingford house burned to the ground."

Doyle looked back at the stage as the music stopped and some kind of altercation between the performers ensued. Marcel's angry screech filled the club. "What I heard is that one of *your* guys torched the place," Doyle said.

"Just tell me your alibi."

"I was out drinking."

"Just you and Jim Kinsey, right?"

"That's right. We hit a dozen places down by the river."

"I hit those same places this morning. Well, those that were open early. People tend to remember you, Doyle, but the odd thing is not one of them recall Kinsey."

"I stand out," Doyle said with a smirk.

Onstage, Marcel launched into a new

tirade directed at his backup dancers, firing them all on the spot. He left in a huff. More music started, and a pop star impersonator took the stage dressed in tiny pink shorts and a halter top, yellow ponytail flying in time to the music.

"So, what are two guys who have no history with each other doing out drinking together on a Monday night?"

"Is there some law—"

Ryan lowered his voice. "You want me to stop tiptoeing, I'll stop tiptoeing. I don't think Kinsey was with you that night. I think he was busy playing with matches. One way or another, I'm going to get him. When I do, I'll call the D.A. You'll get to strut your stuff, only then, it's going to be perjury and that means jail time. You'll come out a felon and that means you won't be able to carry a bullet in your pocket let alone a gun. Hard to be a bodyguard when you can't carry."

Doyle stared straight ahead at Marcel who stood offstage berating a beleaguered man who seemed to be the choreographer.

"How much did Kinsey pay you to cover for him?"

Doyle didn't answer. He kept staring at Marcel while Ryan watched the kid in the halter top gyrating to kinky music most twelve-year-old girls knew by heart.

"You think your boss hasn't noticed you over here having a quiet little tête-à-tête with a cop?" Ryan said. "If the thought of a grand jury doesn't get to you, think about how Marcel's going to interpret seeing you talking to me the day before the OLCC comes a knocking. Suppose he's thrown any after-hour parties lately? Can't do that if you have a liquor license, you know. Can't even drink a beer after closing time. I wonder—"

"One thousand," Doyle said with a grunt. "I don't know nothing about him and the fire. All I know is Kinsey knew I'd been drinking the night before and gave me a big one to tell everyone he was right there by my side. I was between jobs so I took the money. I ain't seen him since."

"A thousand bucks is a lot to spend for an alibi the day after an employer's house goes up in smoke. It never crossed your mind he might be involved?"

"I mind my own business," Doyle said.

"How did he know you were out drinking?"

"I ran into him at the last place I visited, right before closing time."

"And you recognized him?"

"I'd seen him around. I knew who he was."

"I don't suppose he smelled like smoke?"

"I don't suppose so," Doyle said.

"One more thing. Let me see your gun."

This earned him another glance from Doyle. "Why?"

"Just let me see it."

Doyle reached beneath his sports jacket and withdrew a Beretta. Walnut grip, 9mm double action, matte-black finish. Lethal, efficient. But not the gun Tess described, not the nickel-plated revolver her attacker ran up and down her face.

"You better hope I never find out you lied about this," Ryan said, glancing at his watch as Doyle holstered the gun.

If Ryan hurried, he had time to tackle Kinsey before picking up Tess.

TESS FINALLY HAD TO ADMIT the only way she was going to get inside Nelson Lingford's desk was with a crowbar or a shotgun. As neither implement was close at hand, she settled on sitting back in his swivel chair and furrowing her brow. That's when she spied the mail on his desk. She shuffled through a few envelopes from banks and other businesses, stopping to linger over a heavily taped small box wrapped in brown paper. No return address, postmarked New Harbor.

Dare she swipe it or open it?

No. The maid would remember bringing it in here. Irene would recall her absence. She put the box back with the other mail and looked at the computer with lust, wishing she could get into its files, but there was no way she had that kind of time.

Why did spying look so easy in a movie?

Twirling in Nelson's desk chair, she settled with the bottom drawer of the file cabinet, the only drawer not locked. She found a dozen neat-as-a-pin files and began leafing through them. They all appeared to be related to household expenses which, while truly impressive by her modest standards, didn't shed much light on anything.

She checked her watch. She'd been gone almost ten minutes. Time to get back to the dining room before Irene thought she'd locked herself in the bathroom and came looking. But what if Irene saw her leaving the den? She snatched a piece of notepaper. "Sorry to have missed you," she scribbled. She was halfway across the room when the door opened.

Nelson paused at the door, his gaze puzzled when it landed on her. Too late she realized her oversize glasses were in her hand while she'd left her crutches propped against the filing cabinet and was actually in the process of placing her weight on her cast-covered foot.

"I see you're feeling better," he said, closing the door behind him. His lips curved into a smile, but his eyes were as empty as a moonscape.

THE MAN WHO ANSWERED the door at 306 Sand Dollar Court was fifteen years too old to be Jim Kinsey. He also had a horrible cold, evidenced by watery eyes and nose, hacking cough and the box of tissues clutched to his chest.

"Some guy moved out last week," the man said, following the news with a sneeze. He mopped at his nose, looked over Ryan's shoulder and groaned, "God almighty, it's raining again. I don't believe it."

"Any idea where he moved to?"

"No. Never met him. The place had a For Rent sign in the office, and I took it."

Ryan left the man to find the manager's office. A very pregnant woman answered the door, her belly bulging against a shiny red nylon blouse.

"Jim Kinsey is a no-account liar," she said. A small boy of about two wrapped an arm around one of her denim-clad legs, and she absently tousled his hair. "He left in the dead of night, didn't pay his rent, let alone leave a forwarding address."

"Do you know if he had a new job?" Ryan asked, smiling at the little kid who had bravely stepped away from his mother toward Ryan.

"I know he used to drive a fancy car for a lady, but her house burned down and she went to live somewhere else. I read that in the paper. That's when Jim started acting weird."

"Weird? In what way?"

"He stopped going out for a while. I thought maybe he was depressed on account of losing his job. Me and my husband cut him a break with his rent check that month, but then he started bringing girls home which we don't approve of, but what can we do, we're only the managers and he wasn't violating the lease. He bought himself some fancy clothes and a new car but he still didn't pay his rent, and just when Dennis, that's my husband, was going to kick him out of here, he moves out on his own without paying any back rent. We're going to turn him over to our collection agency. If you find him, let us know, okay?"

"I will. You have no idea where he went?"

"Maybe down to Lincoln City. He used to work there, before he was a driver. He was a fireman."

Jolted by this news—it hadn't shown up in the report Ryan had read and reread—he said, "Are you sure? A fireman?" Firemen knew all about setting fires.

"Yeah, I'm sure. He bragged about it to my fifteen-year-old sister, Laurie, when she came up here last summer. Dennis read Jim the riot act and we shipped Laurie home before she could do something stupid."

The little boy was now staring up at Ryan, who suddenly realized his gun was visible in its shoulder holster. He pulled his leather jacket closer around his body, patted the kid, who darted back behind his mother.

"Did he tell Laurie why he wasn't a fireman anymore?"

"Said the chief had it in for him. But he has an awful temper, so I suppose it had something to do with that."

"Is he still in contact with Laurie?"

"Absolutely not. Besides, Laurie moved on when she got back home. Has a new boyfriend and everything."

Ryan handed the woman a card and asked her to get in touch with him if Kinsey contacted her.

Dead end. Plus he was late picking up Tess. But there were sure to be additional contacts in the computer at work linking Kinsey to family and friends. He'd call Donovan and get a list of names and do this the old-fashioned way, by tracking him through the people he cared about, the people whose addresses he'd used at various times.

Ryan was walking out toward the curb when he heard footsteps behind him and turned suddenly, catching a breathless woman in his hands before she collided with him.

"I live in the apartment next to where Jim Kinsey used to live," she said, catching her breath and backing away. "I heard you over there talking to the new guy. You still looking for Jimmy?"

She was about twenty, slightly built with short curly dark hair spilling over her forehead. She wore a black sweater over a gray dress and looked cold. "Yeah, do you know where he is?"

"I might. Why do you want to see him?"

"I have money for him," Ryan said, attempting to look as un-cop like as possible.

"Give me the money and I'll get it to Jimmy," she said.

"Sure you will," Ryan said with a laugh and turning, continued walking to his car.

By the time he put his hand on the driver's door handle, she was standing on the sidewalk, arms around herself, her hair now a halo of frizz. She looked at him across the top of the car. "Okay, I'll tell you where he is but he won't be there right now cause he works till three-thirty."

"Where does he work?"

"He drives a truck for a gravel company. Right now they're taking stuff down the coast. He said he's quitting after today. Said he's about to come into a big hunk of money. Maybe you're the messenger, right?"

"Maybe," Ryan said.

"Jimmy has come into money before and he pisses it away. Buys himself fancy cars and—well, just don't tell him I told you. He'd be furious with me."

"Furious that you're helping him get the

money owed him?" he said, watching her eyes for some sign he was being misled. "That doesn't make sense."

"He's touchy lately. Anyway, he's living in a small house at the rear of a bigger house on English Street. I don't remember the address, but the big house is empty and painted the most awful mustard color. Go through the alley in back. But don't tell Jim I sent you."

"Not a word," Ryan said. "What does he drive?"

"A black SUV. He parks it next to his place."

Ryan smiled to himself as he drove away. It looked as though Katie, by requesting those names, and Tess, by intuitively grasping their significance, had broken open the case. He could see it unpeeling like an onion. He could hardly wait to tell Donovan about it someday.

None of this would salvage Matt Fields's reputation, though. Ryan wished there was a way to save Tess from knowing the whole truth, but he knew there wasn't. He'd just have to be there to pick up the pieces.

If she'd let him.

Chapter Nine

Tess did the first thing that came to mind. She stepped down hard on her supposedly injured leg and crumpled to the floor, crying out in pain, holding her leg, groaning in agony while furtively replacing her glasses.

The wary look on Nelson's face dissolved in the face of her apparent injury. He knelt down beside her, gripping her arm. "Are you all right? What were you doing without your crutches? Shall I call an ambulance?"

"No, no ambulance," she said, trying to look pitiful. Not so hard, not really.

He helped her to a standing position just as Irene rushed into the room. The older woman took in the scene and hurried to Tess's side. "What happened?"

"I thought I could walk without my crutches," Tess mumbled. "I...I came in here to leave Nelson a note. When I was done, I wondered if I was better, if I could walk without the crutches, but I can't. I stumbled right as Nelson came into the room."

She couldn't tell how much of this story Irene believed. Her concern was that Nelson believe her.

His brow wrinkled. "I thought for a moment—"

"You thought what?" Irene said.

"I'm sorry, Caroline. You looked guilty about something. I thought you were snooping."

"The minute I saw you I realized what a fool I was being," Tess said. She took the crutches Nelson handed her. "Okay, that's better. I'm fine. Really, both of you, I'm fine."

"Madeline thought you were gone for the day," Irene said to Nelson.

"I came back for my appointment book," he said. He took his keys from a pocket and unlocked the top desk drawer, retrieved his book and relocked the drawer. Then his eyes landed on the mail and the small box on top of the mail. He picked it up and turned it over. Without looking at either woman, he retrieved his letter opener and sliced through the tape.

Tess could barely believe her luck. Nelson was going to unwrap that box right in front of her! She watched as the paper fell to the desk top and he opened the lid. His expression went from curious to livid as he dropped the box and two charcoal briquettes tumbled onto the wood.

"Where did this come from?" he snapped, staring right at Tess. She flinched.

"Your maid delivered your mail," Irene said. "Ask her."

"Believe me, I will," he said. But Tess got the impression he knew exactly where those charcoal briquettes had come from and why and, furthermore, that he thought she'd had a hand in sending them. Before leaving the back of the desk, Nelson bent down to close the bottom file drawer and once again his angry gaze swept over Tess. She looked away at once, but not before she'd spied the cold assessment in his eyes, the thin line of his mouth.

"My cousin will be here any moment," she said. "I have to go."

"I'll get your bag," Irene said as Tess clumsily used her crutches to leave the den.

"I'll get it," Nelson said.

"It's in the music room."

As soon as Nelson left, Irene whispered, "Are you really okay?"

"I'm fine," Tess said as they entered the foyer. Her voice was shaking, her knees felt wobbly. "My cousin will be here soon. You don't mind if I leave early—"

"Of course not. Frankly, I'm relieved you're getting out of here," she said, helping Tess with her coat. "Who would send Nelson such a weird thing? It worries me to have you here when you're so vulnerable. I wonder what's taking Nelson so long?"

"Here we go," Nelson said, handing Tess her bag, his fingers lingering when their hands touched. Now it was Tess's turn to look suspiciously at Nelson. Had she left the top of her purse unzipped or had *he* been snooping?

Katie's real ID was in the inside pocket.

"I'm sorry I snapped at you," he said. "The maid said the package came with the rest of the mail."

"Of course it did," Irene said. "Who sent it, Nelson?"

"There was no return address—"

"But you know who sent it," she persisted.

"Yeah," he said. "I know who sent it." He looked directly at Tess who made herself meet his gaze. "Maybe we could have dinner tonight," he added.

She wanted to laugh. Have dinner? Who could eat with those cold eyes staring...she could. She said, "Sure."

"I'll pick you up—"

"No, no, I'll meet you at your office," she said, thinking about the trophy. If she could just get her hands on it. Maybe it hid...well, something! A key to a file... something.

"Fine. I have late meetings. Around eight?"

As Tess nodded, she met Irene's gaze. The woman looked worried. Tess longed to reassure her, hating the feeling that she was adding to Irene's burdens.

But she couldn't. Not yet. For now she had to escape this house. Madeline's sudden arrival at the front door, a subdued but recovering Muffy in her lap, gave Tess an opportunity to slip outside in time to see the driver move the hydraulically equipped van around the corner toward the vast garages.

She couldn't help but notice the van was light gray.

"THERE'S A VAN at that house," Tess said excitedly a few minutes later. Ryan had arrived right on time. It had taken a great deal of willpower on her part not to throw her arms around his neck, but anyone could be watching from the windows so she'd kept a respectable distance.

"How could the police miss the fact Nelson Lingford owns a van?" she added.

"Because Nelson Lingford doesn't own a van," Ryan said, leaving the Lingford estate behind them. "Madeline Lingford owns it. And it's gray. Besides, do you honestly picture Mrs. Lingford mowing down Katie?"

"Ah, but remember, Madeline doesn't drive the van, Nelson's driver does. If Nelson wanted Katie mowed down, he'd just give his driver a bonus to do it for him."

"When did you get this cynical?" Ryan asked, his brow furrowed as he glanced at her. "Nelson's driver got investigated just like everyone else. He's a fifty-two-year-old Sunday school teacher. He volunteers at a soup kitchen. He's not the kind to run down an innocent girl just because his boss says run her down."

But Tess couldn't let it go. "What happened that particular day that made it imperative Katie be silenced? I'll tell you what. She met with Nelson. She wanted to know about the insurance investigation and Nelson's whereabouts and she took that photo of his trophy—"

"He probably asked her to take it. To show off for a pretty girl."

"Maybe," Tess said, deciding on the spot not to mention her dinner date. Who knew what the next few hours would reveal? After they looked through Katie's locker—if they found it—almost anything could happen. "But Nelson could have been driving the van for some reason. All we have to do is check out the front bumper."

"The problem," Ryan said, interrupting, "is that since we're flying under police radar, we can't send a team out here to process the van. But I will call around and see if it spent any time in a body shop this week."

"And that could prove Katie's accident wasn't an accident. But first we have to find Katie's storage garage. Oh, wait, I had another thought. What about her car? Maybe she put something in the trunk."

"I checked her car. Nothing there. And you're forgetting something. Katie also went to Irene Woodall's house for a birthday party that day. Maybe Irene is behind all this."

"What would Irene have to gain? As far as

I can see, she lost access to an art collection she loved."

"Maybe she decided if she couldn't have it, no one could."

"Okay. But where would she get all that money to pay an arsonist?"

"That's a problem. She got checked out like everyone else after the fire. Her daughter is taken care of by money she came into once her father died. Irene lives modestly over her shop, employs only one assistant—"

"Two. There's Georges and someone else helping out while Irene babysits Madeline's project. Why does she feel so protective of Katie?"

"I don't know," he said.

"Is there a way Irene could have tapped into the money her husband left for Tabitha? If she's crazy enough to want to destroy the art, maybe she wouldn't worry about how much money Tabitha had left."

"I'll check into it tomorrow," he said.

Tess's thoughts tumbled over one another. "Someone sent Nelson a box with two charcoal briquettes in it. No note that I could see, but he admitted he knew who they were from though he wouldn't say. Interesting, huh? And I also got to thinking about Muffy,

Madeline's dog. It appears Nelson poisoned the dog and delayed treatment. What if he's planning on killing Madeline to get at the few remaining paintings?"

"She made a will after the fire," he said. "She left the fire-damaged art to the museum. The curator is happy to take what she can get. I think Nelson is just clueless when it comes to the dog. Not that he isn't guilty as hell about everything else."

"Wait," Tess said, holding up a finger. "I have another idea. What if someone is black-mailing Nelson and that's why they sent him the briquettes? It's like a threat, you see? If he doesn't pay up, his house will be charcoal or evidence will appear that proves he was responsible for his stepmother's fire."

Ryan stared at her for a second and smiled. "Not bad, Sherlock."

"So who would do that?"

"We'll get all the suspects to line up single file. It could be almost anyone."

Another idea surfaced. "What if Madeline herself is behind all this?"

"Behind all what?"

"The fire, the attacks. Nelson will eventually get the money, but Madeline will get it first. And Madeline is stronger than anyone thinks plus she really is dedicated to Nelson. He's her only family."

"Then why donate the art?" Ryan said. "Besides, why in the world would she destroy her own home?"

"Okay, so she didn't start the fire, she just suspects Nelson did and is covering for him."

"Well, for now, I have a lead on Jim Kinsey, Madeline's former driver. We need to head there before his girlfriend starts regretting her loose lips and decides to warn him someone was asking around." He looked uneasy. Was he nervous about taking her along on a mission he thought would be dangerous?

"I'm a big girl," she said. "And trust me, as long as you're there, I can handle meeting my attacker again. If I can handle that Nelson believes I rifled through his office—"

This earned her a quick glance as Ryan pulled to a stop behind a big beer delivery truck. "You were in his office?"

"I was looking for incriminating evidence, something that linked him to his stepmother's fire. It bothers me that he moved a woman he obviously doesn't like much into his house after that fire, fired her driver, maybe tried to kill the dog who saved her life—anyway, next time I'll get into his computer."

"Don't tell me any of this," he said, all but covering his ears. "You can't go breaking into people's desks and rifling through their computers. It's illegal."

"He didn't catch me," she said, not adding the "at least I don't think he did" that immediately followed that thought.

"It's still illegal."

She nodded absently.

Tess was the first to spot the mustard-colored house on English Street, and the informant was right, it did look empty. The grass needed mowing, the drapes were closed, there were no cars in the driveway. A fence at the front of the property meant they couldn't see the back from the street. Before they attracted the unwanted attention of an older couple walking hand in hand down the sidewalk, Ryan drove around the corner and took a right into the alley.

The smaller house sat almost flush with the alley road. There was a pad of cement next to the tiny structure. No car was parked on the cement.

"This doesn't look like the place a guy

with fifty thousand dollars would choose to live," Tess said.

"It does if he put most of it into clothes, women and cars," Ryan said. "Fifty grand isn't that much money, not when you're into grandstanding. Anyway, we'll come back later when he gets off work. Maybe by then we'll have more information. The first storage garage isn't far."

"Can't we just stop and look in the window or accidentally break a lock—"

"Stop," Ryan said, driving by without pausing as though he thought someone might be watching. "I don't know why you've suddenly become a B and E expert but you have to knock it off."

She laughed. As he took a left out of the alley, he spared her a smile. "What's with you today?"

"I think I'm too scared to be scared."

"Maybe it's just the love of a good man," he said.

She glanced out her window. Had he said the word *love*? After a couple of days and some remarkable sex, he was talking love? That was crazy. He knew that, right?

"Are you hungry?"

"Just anxious about the garage," she said, deciding he'd been joking and she was getting way too touchy. "If the key has a number stamped on it, why can't we just go find the proper unit and see if the key fits?

Ryan had pulled up at the curb in front of a place called Ace Ministorage. Pointing at the gate located between the office and the units, he said, "You're going to have to come up with some story of forgetting their entrance code before we can even try to find the correct locker. Unless you want me to pull my policeman act, and then we run the risk of involving the department—"

"Just stop the car. No troops, not yet."

As they were both sure Katie would have used her own identity, as opposed to that of Caroline Mays, to rent a storage unit, Tess carried Katie's driver's license.

The young woman behind the desk was reading a mystery novel, eating potato chips out of a small bag and guzzling soda out of a can as Tess stood in front of the desk. When the girl finally looked up, it was with the impatient expression of someone who clearly resented being interrupted.

"What do you need?"

"I can't remember the code to get through

the gate. I want to get something out of my garage."

"What's your name?" the girl said, turning down a corner of her book and setting it aside.

"Katie Fields."

The girl popped a chip into her mouth as she scrolled down the computer screen. "Let me see your driver's license," she said.

Tess handed it over. The girl checked the spelling and handed it back to Tess. "I don't have you listed."

"Maybe you have my, uh, sister's name. I mean, maybe she gave you her name when she rented the garage for me—"

"What's her name?"

"Caroline Mays."

The girl rechecked her screen. "Nope. Besides, you're not supposed to do that. Insurance, you know. You have to hand over your ID and then you can name people authorized to visit your unit but—hey, how could you forget which one of you rented storage?"

"I've been in an accident," Tess said.

"Oh. Yeah. Listen," she added, spying the key Tess held in her hand. "Customers use their own locks here. It's really hard to control things if you issue keys. People take the keys when they leave or duplicate them—you're always having to change the locks. Only place I know who still does it like that is Stanley's Storage over on Hawthorne. I don't think he cares if people steal things out of old lockers. Oh, wait, there's another place, a new place called—oh, something with an *X*. Axel or Excel. Something like that. Man, it must have been a bad accident if you can't even remember where you rented a unit."

"Pretty bad," Tess said, hobbling toward the door. "Thanks for your time."

The girl waved Tess away with her book.

"Next we try something called Excel or Axel—" Tess told Ryan as she threw her crutches into the back seat.

"X-Cell," Ryan interrupted. "I saw it in the phone book. It's a few blocks over, toward the river."

"After that there's a place called Stanley's on Hawthorne."

"Never heard of it."

X-Cell was set up like a single-story apartment complex with paved roads between the strings of units, numbered all the way up to two hundred. There was no gate admittance at this faculty, but there was a front office, which Ryan drove past with the authority with which Tess noticed he did just about everything. They found the right row and drove toward the end, stopping when 119 came into sight.

Tess fitted the key in the lock, and they both held their breaths as she turned it.

"No go," she said, but Ryan had to try it for himself and it was a measure of how fond she was growing of him that she allowed him to do so without much irritation. Maybe he'd have a magic cop touch or his superior strength would turn the trick!

But it didn't, and in the end, they had to accept that X-Cell wasn't the right place.

"Might as well try Stanley's. You know where Hawthorne Street is?"

He sent her a dry look that reminded her he'd not only grown up in New Harbor, he was a policeman here and he knew damn near every street.

They finally spotted a slightly lopsided and much rusted sign announcing Stanley's Storage pounded into the ground at the mouth of a narrow gravel road. The road led between an old bowling alley on one side and an even older truck stop on the other. The muddy road eventually ended in a muddy turnaround in front of an aluminum building with twenty separate outside doors. A big mud-spattered truck hooked up to a flatbed trailer occupied a good deal of the parking lot. There wasn't a soul to be seen, nor was there an office or a gate. Stanley's Storage appeared old, decrepit, standing on one leg, so to speak. Tess knew the moment she saw it that it was exactly the kind of place Katie would choose in which to secrete away the artifacts of her old life while she created a new one.

"I hate to state the obvious, but there aren't 119 units here," Ryan said.

What they found were exactly twenty units with the numbers starting at one hundred. Katie's locker, if it was Katie's locker, was the second to the end.

Ryan drove up to the front of it and parked the car. The rain had stopped and for a moment they both sat looking at the corrugated aluminum door.

"You try it," Ryan said at last, looking around him as though expecting half a dozen bad guys to be on their tail.

Before Tess could slide out of her seat, Ryan caught her hand. "Don't get your hopes up too high," he said.

His gray eyes filled with concern as he squeezed her hand.

Hope for what? That there would be a box of cold hard cash in that garage so they could use it to get to the mastermind of this crime? Or hope there was no money. While that fact alone wouldn't salvage her father's reputation, it wouldn't pound another nail in his coffin, either. Tess shuddered at the metaphor that had leaped to mind.

The key fit the lock and the lock turned.

Tess took a deep breath.

Ryan had joined her and now rolled up the door.

The room was packed floor-to-ceiling with boxes so close together they presented a unified wall of cardboard seamed with the tiniest of cracks. The impressive stack began about a foot inside the door and continued on forever, or at least it seemed they did.

"Wow," Ryan said, his voice hushed. "There must be hundreds of boxes in this place."

"We'll never get through them all in time," Tess said, glancing at her watch. It was after two o'clock.

Ryan wiggled his fingers in a slight gap and tried to pull out one of the boxes in the middle, but the fit was too tight and it wouldn't budge.

A loud growling noise caught both their attention at once, and they turned in tandem to see a backhoe crawling along the road from an area behind the building in which they stood. It was carrying a small metal container like those used on container ships.

The backhoe driver was a ruddy man wearing a blue windbreaker and a baseball cap sporting a tractor logo. Grayish hair curled around his cherubic face and damn if his eyes didn't twinkle. He stopped the big piece of machinery in front of Ryan and Tess and turned off the engine. Leaning forward, he said, "Where have you been, young lady? I was getting worried about you. So was Doris. Oh, my gosh, look at you. Are you okay?"

"I was in an accident," Tess said. She fell back on her standby and added, "It left me a little rattled. I don't always remember things."

The man's expression turned sympathetic. "My goodness, Katie, is that a fact?" He looked suspiciously at Ryan and added, "Don't recall you ever coming with her before, young man."

"I'm her cousin, Ryan Hill," Ryan said. "I've been helping Katie. She just today recalled this unit so we came out to make sure the rent was paid and everything was dry after all this rain we've been having."

"Don't worry about that. "We may be a little lackadaisical out this way, but the place is dry and warm, just like advertised and she paid her rent up for four months so there's plenty of time left. Doris will be all torn up to hear you been hurt, Katie."

"Doris?"

"Doris! The wife! Hell, you really did get conked on the head, didn't you?"

"I'm on the mend," Tess said. "Uh, I know this sounds nuts, but you're making it sound as if I came here off and on once I rented the unit."

"All the time," the man said. He'd finally straightened up and Tess could see an embroidered name over his chest pocket. She was apparently talking to Stanley himself. "Two or three times a week."

Tess looked at the wall of boxes and said, "What did I do here?"

He shook his head and smiled. "Don't rightly know. I'm not a spy. Besides, you rolled the door closed after yourself and as you paid the rent it weren't none of my business. But ever so often you come back to the office where the wife does the books and I loaf around when I'm not moving these containers around and ate some of the wife's cookies. She thought you were lonely."

Tears stung Tess's eyes.

"Now don't go crying," Stanley said. "Doris will hit me over the head with a file cabinet if she hears I made you cry.

"It's okay," Ryan said as he put a brotherly arm around Tess's shoulders.

"There's fresh coffee and peanut butter cookies if you've got the time," Stanley said.

"I can't today," Tess said. "I'd like to another time, though."

"Anytime you want and that's a fact," Stanley said warmly. He nodded at Tess, turned the key, and the tractor roared. Tess watched him rumble back the way he'd come with a bittersweet smile on her lips.

Stanley didn't know it, but he'd just given her a new glimpse of her sister. A woman devastated by loss who apparently looked through her things two or three times a week, a woman who ate cookies with a middle-aged couple and who struck them as lonely.

Once again she silently sent the message: *Katie, wake up!* But this time it wasn't sent with desperation. This time it was sent with love.

"We've got thirty minutes or so to find fifty thousand dollars," Ryan said. "I guess we'd better get started."

Chapter Ten

"The trouble is we have no proof Jim Kinsey is your father's accomplice."

Beside him, she stiffened, he supposed at his choice of words. They'd relocked the storage garage after tackling a row or two of boxes and finding nothing but clothes on top and books below.

This was one of those enigmatic things he found so head-shakingly compelling about Tess. On the one hand she would stand there and swear her father had to be innocent, framed. Of course there was no pay-off money, she'd argue, because her father hadn't done anything except be at the wrong place at the wrong time.

On the other hand, she searched through dozens of books looking for hidden bills— just in case. She was a thoughtful, intelligent woman when it came to anyone but the father and sister she hadn't known existed a few days before. With them she struggled to believe in their perfection one hundred percent.

Didn't she understand no one was one hundred percent anything?

"From what you told me about this Kinsey guy, he sounds like a perfect candidate for the arson," Tess said.

They were parked a few houses down from the big mustard-colored house fronting Kinsey's place. According to Kinsey's girlfriend, Kinsey got off work at 3:30 p.m. and it was almost that now.

Ryan said, "If so, it's just a matter of breaking him to discover which of our suspects paid him to start the fire."

"How does my father fit in? Where's the connection to Lingford or Doyle or Kinsey or Irene or Madeline or Desota...did I miss anyone?"

"I don't know, but it's there. What we know for sure is there's one force attempting to recover fire money from Katie Fields and another force scared of what the new woman in Nelson Lingford's life might discover, again Katie, only this time masquerading as Caroline."

Ryan fell silent as he tried to get the facts straight in his head. Over Tess's shoulder, he watched a man in a tan raincoat and a colorful blue-and-white neck scarf saunter down the opposite sidewalk. The man carried a shopping bag under his arm. He exchanged a greeting with an older woman standing on the porch of a royal-blue house shaking out a rug. Coming the other direction, two boys on bikes sped along the sidewalk, darting into the street to avoid the walker without glancing behind them.

Kids. The neighborhood reminded Ryan of the kind in which he and Peter and his sisters had been raised. A good place for kids and older people, nothing like he'd ever envisioned for himself. So why did he all of a sudden feel a flicker of interest in this domestic scene?

He glanced at Tess, who was deep in thought, and knew why. It was her. Right at the beginning she'd asked him if he believed in love at first sight and because she so obviously thought it was nuts, he'd said no. The truth was he wasn't sure. Besides, this wasn't first sight, this was many sights later and all he knew for certain was that it was increasingly difficult to imagine a future without Tess Mays at its hub.

Did he love her? Heaven help him, he thought maybe he did. But he knew she didn't love him. Not yet....

"*Assuming* you're right," Tess said, "what now? Do we wait for Kinsey to call and arrange a drop-off?"

"I love it when you talk cop," he said, leaning forward and kissing her.

She looked startled by his kiss, seemed to shrug off its impact like a duck sheds water. "I was wondering. What about the paintings recovered from the fire? Have they been authenticated?"

"You're thinking someone could have stolen the art and then burned down the house as a ruse? Donovan said that was their first thought, too. The insurance company would love to prove it. But the restoration company in charge of the few remaining paintings confirms their authenticity, plus witnesses outside the family put the entire collection in place as late as the very afternoon before the fire."

Tess wrinkled her brow as she thought. "She's a lot stronger than she looks," Tess said after a moment.

"Who?"

"Madeline Lingford. She moves pretty quickly when the mood hits her."

"The wheelchair thing is real. The woman was in an accident years ago. Her first husband died in the crash. Despite all the pampered care she receives, she still does a lot for herself and that's why she's strong."

"Did you check her out?"

"Thanks to HIPPA her medical records are sealed. We have no reason to subpoena them. Anyway, let's concentrate on step one and that's interviewing Kinsey although I'm wondering if Doyle found out what Kinsey did and decided to cut himself in. Let's see. We have your dad acting as a torch or lookout, Kinsey with a knowledge of fires and some third party paying for the job. Oh, and then there's whoever is searching Katie's apartment."

Tess nodded woodenly. Despite her banter, Ryan saw fatigue etched on her face. They'd made love half the night and then spent a long day gathering facts and he'd just blatantly mentioned her father's guilt. She hadn't protested. She looked bushed. And terrified.

He made a snap decision and started the car. He drove around the block, pulling to a stop at the end of the alley. From this vantage point, he could see the shiny black SUV parked kitty-corner on the cement slab.

"And that's where Kinsey put his first fifty grand," Ryan said. "In that car. Look at the chrome. Well, at least we know he's home. I guess he left work early." Ryan glanced at Katie's cell phone resting on the counsel between them. "Why don't you give him a call and see what he has to say?" He dug a scrap of paper out of his pocket. His partner, Jason, had given him Kinsey's number off an arrest sheet for a DUI made a few days before.

"No!" Tess said at once. "I don't want to talk to him yet. I have to psych myself up first. Let him call us."

Ryan leaned across the gearshift knob and gently kissed her panic away. "I'll call," he said. "We don't have the money. It's time to change the game plan."

She'd closed her eyes when he kissed her, a gesture that made something funny happen in his chest. "Shouldn't we wait?" she murmured.

"I hate waiting," he said, smoothing a strand or two of her brilliant red hair behind her ear, longing for the day when it would again be blond, when she'd look at him without fear in her eyes, when he could talk to her about something other than their current predicament. Another constriction in his chest—not a heart attack, at least not the medical kind. He pictured his poor old heart ratcheted from his open chest like the engine out of a car, hanging above him, a big ponderous, sorry-looking thing, horribly exposed, yearning for a chance at happiness. Face it, if he proved Tess's father guilty without a doubt, she might cut his heart free to crash back into its hiding place.

He rubbed his eyes. Maybe she wasn't the only tired one. Picking up the phone, he said, "Don't say a word, I don't want Kinsey to know you're here with me in this car."

"But what are you going to say?"

"I'm going to make him a deal he can't refuse." One look at Tess's troubled face, and Ryan relented a little. "I'm going to tell him we're having trouble getting the money and need another day. I'm going to let him know I'm watching him so he doesn't get any funny ideas about hurting you or Madeline Lingford or the grump. I'll tell him that when we find the money he's welcome to it, all he has to do is give us one little name and leave you and everyone else here alone."

"Why would he agree to that?"

"Because he's greedy. He could have killed you already if he wanted to. He doesn't want you dead, and he doesn't want you so angry you call the cops. He doesn't think you know who he is. Once he figures out I'm on to his identity and willing to pay up to get rid of him, he'll wait a few more hours for the payoff. If I were him and I was playing the middle against the ends, I'd be hankering to leave town, wouldn't you?"

"You don't know any of that for certain."

"Nothing's for certain," he agreed.

He punched in the right numbers. The phone rang and rang.

"Maybe he's asleep," Tess whispered.

"Yeah, maybe. Or maybe he's not even home. Stay here while I make sure his place only has one door. Keep the car locked."

Before she could react, he got out of the car and ran back to the main street, approaching the house from the side, going through a neighbor's yard, peering over a hedge. He could see the back and the north side of Kinsey's place from this vantage point. No doors.

He ran back to the car. "Okay, keep your head low. It's time to check out Kinsey."

He started the engine and drove down the alley, parking in back of the SUV, blocking its path of escape. The other two sides of the small house were visible. The door opened onto the alley. Despite the car, the place looked deserted.

"Stay here," Ryan said as he eased open his door and got out. To avoid making any noise, he didn't close his door completely. He drew his gun and, holding it up against his chest, moved toward the small house. He touched the hood of the SUV—cold.

So what brought Jim Kinsey home early? The promise of fifty thousand dollars? Maybe the man planned on taking the money and running, maybe the girl at the apartment house was about to be left high and dry and didn't know it yet.

The house itself was tidy but extremely small, painted the same color as the big house. There wasn't much of a yard though a vigorous hedge surrounded three sides. As the door was closed and the drapes were drawn, Ryan found himself at an impasse when it came to further snooping.

He was considering his options for

getting inside without breaking the law when Tess came up beside him, hugging herself, biting her lip.

"I'm not going to be afraid of him," she announced in a whisper, her voice wavering.

"Good."

"I mean it. He's probably the one who scared the daylights out of me yesterday, but today I have you and you have that big gun. Shoot him if he gets near me, okay? Let's knock."

And with that, she reached across his chest and pounded on the door. What the woman lacked in experience, she made up for with bravado. Her pounding brought no answering noise from inside the house. The place was small; if someone was home, it wouldn't matter if they'd been asleep, they'd be awake now. Anyway, does a man getting ready to collect fifty thousand dollars at gunpoint take a nap?

If Kinsey was home, he knew they were at the door. Bullets went right through doors. Ryan turned to knock Tess out of the way if he had to, but she was already in motion. Not bound by his considerations about observing the law, or his gut feeling that Kinsey could blast through that door at any second, she turned the knob and waltzed into the house.

The door led directly into a small square living area that was dark due to the draped windows, but light came through the open door, flooding the area in front of it.

And center stage in the light was a man, face purple, dead eyes bulging, swollen tongue protruding from between lifeless lips, a black cord all but buried in the tight skin of his neck.

Tess stopped in her tracks and gasped.

Gun raised, Ryan stepped in front of her, one arm twisted, clutching her hip as she buried her face against his back.

The dead man sat slumped in a red chair, the only piece of upholstered furniture in the room. Next to him, a straight-back chair looked as though it had been dragged out of the kitchen. A bottle of cheap whiskey sat on a small round table between the chairs. A glass, half-empty, sat beside the bottle. A second glass seemed to have rolled out of Kinsey's hand and landed by his right foot. He wore black boots, caked with mud, black jeans, a denim shirt.

In a heartbeat, Ryan's gaze took in the murky details of the rest of the room. An unmade bed in one corner topped with a navy-blue duffel bag, stuffed with clothes. Clean jeans and a sweater on the bed, loafers nearby on a rug. A jacket draped the closet doorknob. Drawers open and empty, closet likewise.

It looked as though Jim Kinsey had been packing for a trip.

Then what? A knock on the door? Entry of someone he trusted? A shared drink, a sudden strangling?

There were no signs of forced entry, no signs of a struggle. What healthy, burly thirty-year-old man allowed himself to be strangled without putting up a fuss?

Ryan turned to face Tess, gun reholstered, his hands gripping her shoulders. Her cheeks were stained with tears, her expression horrified.

"It's him," she said, her voice shaking as her gaze met Ryan's. "It's the man from yesterday. I recognize his boots. One of them has a brown shoelace. I noticed that yesterday when he stepped on my handbag."

Ryan glanced over his shoulder at the dead man's feet. He saw a brown lace on the right boot, a black one on the left.

"I wanted him dead," she said, voice quivering, eyes averted. "He terrified me and I wanted him dead—"

He squeezed her shoulders. "Don't do this to yourself. You're not responsible. Let's get out of here. Don't touch anything."

Neither of them had advanced far into the room, so it was a short walk back outside. Ryan took care not to touch the knob or anything else.

"We'll call this in from the car," he said, already dreading the hours to come. They assumed the dead man was Kinsey, but a positive identification would come later. If it was indeed Kinsey, then his relation to the Lingfords was public knowledge. He was the fired driver of Madeline Lingford's van. His boots connected him to the violent threats made against Tess posing as Katie. The money he demanded tied him to the fire and also to Tess's dad, killed in the fire.

So, who killed him? The obvious culprit? Nelson Lingford, but it was hard to picture Nelson driving over here, drinking cheap booze and doing his own dirty work. It was hard to picture Nelson overpowering Kinsey, though he was probably in tip top shape. Tess had mentioned windsurfing. It took muscles in the upper arms to windsurf.

Of course, there was always the shadowy third party, but he'd put his money on Nelson.

Tess was visibly shaking and he ran his hands up and down her arms. "It's time to bring in the troops," he said.

TESS SAT IN RYAN'S CAR as darkness stole over the alley. The scene became a maze of police cars, men and women in uniforms, flashing lights and yellow crime scene tape. At one point she accepted a cup of coffee and a blanket from someone. An hour later she was visited by a swarthy man with a dark mustache who told her his name was Detective Sanchez and would she please tell him exactly what happened.

She lost track of Ryan until he knocked on her window. She opened her door.

"I'm going to be awhile," he said.

Bathed by the car's interior light, Ryan's face looked tired, his eyes weary. Would he be standing here at the home of a murder victim if it wasn't for Katie, if it wasn't for her?

Doubtful.

"Is the dead man...was he Kinsey?"

"Yeah," Ryan said. "One of the officers remembered him from the investigation after your father died."

She nodded woodenly.

"Sanchez said he talked to you already," Ryan continued. "He'll probably want to talk to you again tomorrow, but I got permission for you to leave tonight. Take my car." He handed her a scrap of paper and added, "This is my home address. It's four blocks east of the hospital. There's an all-night gas station on the south corner. They can give you directions if you get lost. Look for a gray building with black trim. I'm on the second floor, Apartment 6. The keys are on the ring with the car key. Go to my place. My pal fixed Katie's door again but, please, don't go back there."

"There's no way in hell I'd go back there," she said with a visible shudder.

"Good."

"What are you going to tell Sanchez about me taking over Katie's investigation?"

He slid into the car next to her and closed the door, his face lost in shadows. "I already gave Sanchez a rundown. He'll divulge the information when and if it becomes necessary. What did you tell him?"

"That I was Matt Fields's other daughter,

the one no one knew about. I told him Katie couldn't accept the verdict that our father had been responsible for the fire so she launched her own investigation using our mother's name as a cover. I told him when the police declined to investigate Katie's accident as a premeditated crime, you agreed to help me."

"Good. Right now he's focused on finding who killed Jim Kinsey. All this information is pivotal because it may supply motive for the murder. Or maybe it won't. Maybe it'll turn out the guy put the move on someone else's kid sister who then decided to put an end to Kinsey's philandering. Kinsey's murder is Sanchez's priority."

"What's your priority?" she asked.

"Keeping you alive. Period."

She slipped her hand into his and admired his profile as he looked down at their linked hands. But once again there was that little tug-of-war between her physical need of him and her head telling her to back away. He turned to face her, and before she knew it, he was kissing her. The touch of his tongue against hers sent shivers racing up and down her spine.

He moved away again. "I probably won't be home until daybreak."

She was relieved in a way. She needed time.

"I doubt Clive will actually allow you to see him, but will you sprinkle some kibble in his bowl and check his water?"

"Your cat? Sure."

"And keep my bed warm?"

She smiled at the sudden husky tone of his voice and her own leaping libido. And inside she frowned at the intimacy, the developing need she could feel to be there with him, for him.

He kissed her again before stepping outside the car. Her last glimpse of him was in the rearview mirror, a tall man standing in an alley, backlit by police lights, raindrops shining off the shoulders of his black leather jacket, sparkling in his hair, hands on hips, staring after her.

TESS STOPPED by the hospital first, drawn there by something she couldn't name. She parked the car in the underground garage and raced down the halls to Katie's room, parting the curtain with a feeling she would find her sister sitting up in bed, staring back at her.

But Katie remained supine with eyes closed. For a while, Tess held her sister's limp hand. She closed her eyes and tried to establish a psychic link. She figuratively roamed the back labyrinth of her own mind, keeping herself open to the spark of another consciousness.

But in the end, there was nothing in the back of Tess's mind except the wearying details of the day and the shocking memory of Jim Kinsey's ugly death. She laid her sister's hand back by her side, leaned forward and kissed her brow.

"Wake up soon," she whispered against her cool, dry skin.

A glance at the clock stunned her. It was only a little past eight. Tess used the phone book at the hospital to look up Nelson Lingford and found a business address located only a few blocks away.

They had a dinner date.

Ryan would kill her if he knew she tried to keep it.

But would Nelson be in his office if he'd just murdered Jim Kinsey? Of course not. So, if he was there, wouldn't that prove—

It would prove nothing. It wasn't hard to imagine Nelson killing someone and then taking a woman to dinner. Caution said lock herself away, play it safe, but caution didn't have her curiosity. The photograph of the trophy bugged Tess. Katie had taken it for a purpose. Tess dug in her purse, retrieved the phone and scrolled through the menu. The entire photo gallery was empty!

Who had emptied it? Who'd had an opportunity that day to handle her phone? The obvious choice was Ryan...he'd had the phone for hours the day before. Might he have purposely fooled around with the photos? Why? Who else, then? Irene? Nelson? The only one she could be certain hadn't emptied it was Muffy.

She drove Ryan's car to Nelson's office building, parking on the street, shaking with a combination of aftershock, cold and fear. Wind swept down the wet sidewalk as she walked to the glass doors. She shook the metal handles in frustration.

And as she stood there peering inside at the gloomy lobby, she heard a pinging sound, a whiz, and a small explosion next to her ear.

She stared at the round hole in the glass beside her head. It took a stunned second before it finally dawned on her she was being shot at. Her first instinct was to turn around. A man stood across the street, gun raised. She flew across the sidewalk and ducked behind Ryan's car as another bullet hit the building behind her.

Bullets!

She reached up and grasped the passenger door handle, easing the door open. Would she have the nerve to get inside the car, exposing her head to the gunman?

Who in the world would shoot at her?

She heard a sound and looked down the street in time to see a car approaching. If she timed it right…

The car drove by too quickly. She wasn't ready to make a move, in fact, it seemed she was glued to the concrete. Another noise, another car. This time she waited until the passing vehicle was almost abreast, then thrust herself into the seat and slammed the door. The keys were already in her hand and she jammed them into the ignition, crouching down on the seat. She knew she was the only car parked on the block so she gunned the engine and took off without merging from the parking lane. She heard more pinging against the back of the car and finally looked over the wheel in time to plow into a row of garbage cans set out at the curb.

She was shaking so hard it was hard to

hold on to the steering wheel. She checked the rearview mirror a million times, looking for headlights, not seeing any. The gunman must have been on foot. She made a few detours to make sure she wasn't being followed before finding Ryan's apartment building.

It was relatively small, built on a hillside and surrounded by an amazing amount of trees considering its midtown location. In light of what had just happened, too many trees. The wind heightened the sensation that a horde of bad guys—or one lone gunman— awaited her next move, hidden by the shadows of waving branches.

She parked on the street and tried to calm down, finally darting from the car to the apartment as fast as she could, climbing the stairs in a flash, crutches forgotten in the car. All she wanted to do was get inside.

She found the right number and opened the door quickly, slipping inside the dark, empty apartment, fumbling with the lock, reaching for the light switch, heart leaping to her throat when something twined around her leg.

The cat.

She finally found the light switch and

looked down to find a trim black cat gazing up at her with eyes the color of amber.

"Oh, Clive, you scared me," she said, picking him up and holding him close under her chin. She leaned back against the wall and closed her eyes. Eight or nine pounds of muscle and fur, Clive rubbed her jaw and produced a raspy purr.

"And Ryan said you were standoffish," she scoffed, liking the feel of him. Holding animals was a daily occurrence in what she'd begun thinking of as her "real" life. Clive's healthy, vibrating, warm body was like a balm to her edgy nerves. He meowed as he kneaded claws in midair.

She put him back on the floor and slipped off her shoes and the fake cast. The coat came next, draped over the back of a black leather chair. Then she wandered away from the bright light of the entry toward a dark rectangular window that took up most of the north wall.

The view from the window was amazing. New Harbor wasn't a huge town but what there was of it glowed and glittered with lights. There was a dark stretch farther away—the ocean, no doubt.

But she made a dandy target standing in

that big, open window, so she closed the drapes and looked at the dimly lit apartment around her.

A pair of weights sat in one corner and helped explain Ryan's muscles. Small television, nice stereo and a rack of CDs. A computer desk tucked against one wall, a book case against another. A framed photo caught her eye and she walked over to it, smiling as she recognized a young Ryan standing next to his car. The smile faded as she realized it wasn't Ryan she was looking at. Too short. Hair too light.

Peter.

Clive meowed again, this time from a dark doorway. Tess entered the kitchen, switching on the light over the stove to find Clive's supplies and feed him. Suddenly hungry herself, she opened Ryan's refrigerator. Two small tubs of fruit-flavored yogurt, some cheese, a few vegetables, condiments and a six-pack of beer. Freezer empty. She took one of the yogurts, rooted around in the drawers for a spoon and ate it standing up, leaning against the counter, wishing it was ice cream. After she washed her spoon, she went searching for Ryan's bedroom, using as little light as possible. The feeling of someone outside looking in wouldn't go away.

A dark-red bedspread was the one strong note of color in his bedroom. Two fishing poles leaned together in a corner, a gun safe glinted from the open closet. She stood at the doorway while Clive rubbed her shin. What was she doing hiding here in this man's home?

Should she call the police and report the shooting? She'd been arguing this since getting inside Ryan's place. Logic said call. But fear stilled her hand every time she came close to picking up the phone.

Who would shoot her? Why? Were they shooting at Katie or Caroline or had someone discovered her true identity? It was like a jigsaw puzzle with missing pieces and she finally decided to wait for Ryan and tell him about the shooting.

Ryan. He'd be home soon. He'd be hers.

The truth was that Tess hadn't had many love affairs in her twenty-seven years. She'd dated little during college and not that much since graduating and starting her career. There never seemed to be time.

This thing with Ryan had come on so strong and fast that it was almost as frightening as being shot at. She was aware that she'd instigated some of it, she'd never discouraged him. She couldn't deny the strength of their physical attraction. It was there. It was real.

Or was it?

She took a shower in Ryan's bathroom, wrapped herself in one of his towels, dug through a drawer to find a T-shirt to wear to bed, all the time feeling like an intruder. All so cozy and intimate and terrifying.

Clive joined her in the big bed, making a nuisance of himself.

"You're lonely," she told the cat who purred louder than ever and put a paw on her hand. He loved having his ears scratched and rubbed her finger with one of his fangs.

The phone rang as she was almost asleep and for a second she wondered if she should answer it. What if it was Ryan's mother or one of his sisters? What would she say to them?

How likely they would call in the middle of the night? More likely it was Ryan himself. Shifting the cat aside, she answered the phone.

"I wanted to make sure you got there okay," he said, and his voice sounded so tired that she decided to wait to tell him about the shooting. Maybe it was unrelated. Cities had crime. People got shot. The gunman was sure to be gone, what could Ryan do now that he couldn't do in a few hours?

"I'm fine," she said. Clive repositioned himself and she added, "I like your cat."

"He let you see him?"

"See him? I can't get rid of him. He's currently lying on my chest staring into my eyes. He weighs a ton when he lies like this."

"There's nothing for it, I'm going to have to marry you," he said.

The comment was made flippantly, but it hung for a second too long before he added, "I don't know when I can get back. Make yourself at home."

"Do you know anything yet?

"Not that I can tell you, especially not on a phone. We'll talk later today. Stay safe, Tess."

Safe. As in away from bullets.

She hung up the phone and stared at the cat for a second before switching off the light. And then she lay awake in the dark, unable to sleep, worried about Ryan.

Once or twice now he'd said the word *love*, and just as many times, he'd mentioned marriage. All jokingly, but she'd known him just a short while, and in her world, things like love and marriage didn't happen overnight.

Except to her mother, of course.

Ryan and she were two adults with two lives living in two cities. More to the point, they'd met under strained, difficult circumstances and been thrown together in an unrealistic, crazy manner that would sooner or later resolve itself leaving them what—lovers? Boyfriend, girlfriend? Ships that passed in the night?

And yet she craved him, more of him than he had the time to give, more with each passing moment.

And she couldn't escape the feeling that the reason she craved him was that she was scared. There was a murderer on the prowl and Ryan knew what to do about murderers. She didn't.

And how about him? He was obviously heavily burdened by guilt. Guilt over his brother's death, guilt over his partner's role in an arson, guilt over putting Katie off until she was hurt, and now guilt over Tess being attacked.

Guilt.

Great motivator, lousy building block.

Where in the world was her flaky mother when Tess needed her? Off on a honeymoon with a man she'd only known three weeks before marrying him. Fallen off the face of the earth.

Tess squeezed her eyes shut. Since when had she gone running home to her mother for advice? Since when hadn't she had the brains to make her own decisions? Since when had she lost her identity?

Since meeting Ryan Hill. Since taking on this insane challenge. Since turning her back on who and what she was, acting all clingy and needy, being frightened and weepy, trying to be brave like Katie without even knowing if Katie was brave.

This wasn't her.

Okay.

She could stay in Ryan's bed, waiting for him, tacitly agreeing with his shaky fantasy.

Or she could leave this safe cocoon and venture out into the night. Out with the gunman and the murderer.

The answer rang clear in Tess's head.

Get out of Ryan's bed.

Chapter Eleven

She took his phone off the hook in case Ryan called again. She didn't want him to hear it ringing and ringing and get worried. She wrote him a note and left the apartment. It was the middle of the night and she didn't have the slightest idea where to go.

Back to Katie's apartment? No way.

To the hospital?

No.

But the answer came as she decided against the hospital—she would go to Katie's storage garage.

Driving in the dark in a strange city was not Tess's idea of a good time. Had those headlights in the rearview mirror been there too long? Taken the same twists and turns as she? Where was the storage facility, anyway? Why hadn't she paid closer attention when Ryan drove there?

She passed a diner that looked familiar and turned left, then a tire shop and an auto wrecking place. These all looked familiar. When she found herself coming up on the dimly lit sign for a bowling alley, she slowed down. There was the rusted sign: Stanley's Storage. She made a hard right down the rutted roadway, pulling to a stop in front of 119. She turned off the headlights and turned in the seat, looking out toward the road to make sure no one had followed.

The bowling alley parking lot was dark, but a series of overhead fixtures in the truck stop cast ambient light over a good part of Stanley's road; it appeared blissfully empty.

Taking the flashlight out of the glove compartment, Tess locked the car behind her and opened Katie's unit, glad to be battling wind instead of rain.

Ryan had restacked the first few boxes they'd searched, so Tess chose the other end of the stack to begin her new search. Reaching up on tiptoe, she angled for a grip on the bottom edge of the top box. She'd seen Ryan do this and it had worked after a fashion, though she'd been there to help him as the box began to fall. Anticipating the weight, she braced one arm against the wall and pulled.

Instead of the top boxing sliding forward by itself, all four boxes in the stack moved together. She pulled. They got stuck on a piece of wood sticking out from the wall and as Tess relaxed against them for a moment, they slid backward. Flashing her light, she saw they were taped together and pushed them ahead of her, waiting for them to jam against the next row in back but they didn't. They just kept sliding along the cement floor until they cleared the other boxes and stood independently as a stack.

Tess took the flashlight out of her pocket and shone it into what turned out to be the main cavity of the storage unit.

Katie's secret.

A home away from home. A home she could enter without Stanley and his wife knowing what she was doing. Privacy, a sanctuary.

Tess moved the flashlight slowly, illuminating sections of the unit in a clockwise direction. In one corner lay a single mattress covered with a quilt that stopped Tess's heart. She had a quilt exactly like this, all shades of blue and purple flowers stitched together with pink yarn. Her mother had made it when she was a baby; apparently she'd made two and left one for Katie.

Paintings on the walls, a small lamp beside the bed, books stacked on a shelf along with picture albums and framed photos, a radio next to the lamp. There were two wooden chairs, a freestanding rack of clothes with shoes beneath, boxes of what looked like letters. A suitcase tied with bright scarves, no doubt holding clothes to be cycled into the Caroline wardrobe.

Katie's life.

Tucked away where she could visit it. Hidden from everyone.

Tess returned to close the big rolling door and snap the inside lock before sitting on the bed and turning on the lamp. A soft light filled the unit and Tess used it to examine the photographs on the shelf and those in the album, lingering over shots of her father with his arms around Katie, and those of Katie laughing with friends, pictures so like the ones Tess had of herself with her friends that she found it hard to remember that these pictures weren't of her own youth.

She found a modest stash of candy in a small box on the floor and helped herself to a chocolate bar, biting her lip as she peeled away the paper. It looked as though she and Katie tackled stress in the same way.

Eventually, she lifted the suitcase onto the bed. It was way too heavy for clothes, and a premonition swept over her.

The money.

And there, under a layer of silky scarves, were stacks of bills, more cash than Tess had ever seen at one time, thousands of dollars.

Fifty thousand, she suspected.

An hour later she knew: exactly fifty thousand dollars.

Think, she mumbled, pressing her knuckles against her temples.

The amount couldn't be a coincidence. Katie didn't have this kind of money. That meant she either found it after her father died or he gave it to her before the Lingford fire.

Either way, without knowing Kinsey had also received this exact amount, would Katie have known what to make of it? Probably not. Unless there was another puzzle piece missing.

How had Kinsey found Katie? If he'd known all along about the Caroline persona, would he have waited so long to approach her? No way, he'd be afraid she'd spend the money or turn it over to the police. The searches started the same day Katie was run over, at least as far as Tess knew. Did that mean something?

Tess had counted the money from the suitcase into an empty box. She covered the money with the scarves, closed the flaps on the box and shoved it against the others, closed the suitcase and put it on top of the box, then sat back on the mattress, knees even with her chin.

"Okay, Katie," she whispered. "What's going on?"

And then she knew she needed to see Katie's notebook again. There was something in it if she could just remember what. She had to go back to Katie's apartment.

RYAN TAPPED the top of the blue-and-white squad car. "Thanks for the lift," he called to the patrolman through the open window. He looked around for his car and didn't see it. Tess must have had to park on the next block and walk back.

He climbed the stairs, distracted by the night's events and by his growing need to see and hold Tess in his arms. He could tell her it was over and she was safe. He couldn't tell her her father was innocent of wrongdoing, and he regretted that. He was banking on the fact that she'd known all along her father was guilty, she just hadn't been able to abandon hope.

The apartment was quiet when he entered, and with weak morning sunlight coming through the north window, the place was a study in grays and blacks. Clive, a dark shape against the wall, meowed once, and he leaned down to run a hand along the cat's sleek back.

He walked down the short hall to the bedroom, heart beating faster with every step, anticipating how Tess would look in his bed, hair tousled on his pillow. For one blink of an eye he tried to remember the last woman who had spent the night in his place and couldn't. Lately his life had become a blur of work; he was ready for a change.

Would Tess go on a trip with him? This mess was next door to over. Once they made sure Katie was okay, would Tess consider traveling to an island somewhere? Warm sand. Warm water. Very little in the way of clothing. Long nights. Good wine, all the chocolate chip pancakes she could eat, time to lie in the sun and think about nothing.

He felt the tiredness wash away. Tess was on the other side of the door. He'd take a shower and join her, waking her in the best possible manner—

The fantasy vanished. The bed was neatly made, the bathroom had a steamy warm fragrance that made him smile. He went looking for Tess.

He found her in the living room, fully dressed, asleep in one of his leather chairs, feet propped up on a matching ottoman, a shoe box on her lap. She seemed to sense him staring at her and opened her eyes as though she'd just closed them a few minutes before.

"What did you find out?" she asked without missing a beat.

"Lots," he said, taking the ottoman she'd vacated when she put her feet on the floor and sitting down right in front of her. Clive trotted off to the kitchen.

"There are prints on the extra glass and the bottle. Not Kinsey's prints."

"Then whose?"

"We'll know later. I'm betting Lingford's. The medical examiner is speculating at this point, but he's pretty sure Kinsey's whiskey glass held barbiturates."

"Barbiturates. You mean Kinsey was drugged before he was strangled?"

"From the lack of defensive wounds and signs of a struggle, it looks that way. Here's the good part. Detective Sanchez is on his way over to talk to Lingford right now."

"Because?"

"Two reasons. One, his car was spotted in the neighborhood this afternoon. In fact, do you recall the woman in the blue house who was shaking out her rug when we were parked out on the street?"

She shook her head. "No."

"That's right, your back was to her as well as to the guy walking by. Well, we questioned the neighbors, of course, to see if anyone had seen or heard anything unusual. The officer who questioned this woman said she saw a fancy silver car with a bumper sticker that stuck in her mind. A blue triangle and an orange ball. The triangle, up close, represents a windsurfing sail. The orange ball is the sun."

"And Lingford loves windsurfing."

"This particular logo belongs to a California club."

"Which I assume Nelson is a member of?"

"We'll know pretty soon."

"So, Lingford was in Jim Kinsey's neighborhood?"

"Not only that, but the same witness says a man she didn't know waved at her yesterday afternoon somewhere between three and four. I actually saw him wave. I assumed they were neighbors, but she says now she'd never seen him before."

"Could she identify him?"

"We'll take her pictures to look at. I'm betting it was Nelson. That he parked on a side street and walked to Kinsey's, killed him, then sauntered through the gate out onto the sidewalk and down the street, back to his car."

"So what happens next?"

"More investigation, more questions. If Lingford's fingerprints are on the extra glass on Kinsey's table, it places him at the scene. If he holds a prescription for barbiturates, it's going to look really bad."

"What was Kinsey strangled with?"

"One of his own drapery cords. It's missing from the front window. And, Tess, you have to know they found papers in with Kinsey's things. He kept notes about his bookie. I recognized the name—it's the same guy your father used. That's a connection between the two men."

"I found another connection," Tess said, her gaze shifting away from his.

"What do you mean?"

"I...I couldn't sleep. I didn't stay here. I went to Katie's storage unit."

My God, he thought as he ran a hand through his hair, weariness descending like a fog bank. This woman was hopelessly reckless. The proof she'd survived her trek across town while Nelson Lingford remained at large sat in front of him, but didn't she have any sense at all? Clenching his jaw to keep from saying something he'd regret, he waited.

"The boxes at the right were taped together to make a sort of sliding door. Behind them the unit is more or less open space. She'd made herself a little cave back in there with a mattress and clothes and candy. Someplace she could retreat to when pretending to be Caroline got to be too much. Someplace safe."

Still he waited. He knew what was coming.

"And I found a suitcase full of money. Fifty thousand dollars."

He nodded. "Where's the money?"

"Still in the garage. In a box."

"Okay. Try this on for size. Nelson wants

the art money. He hires his stepmother's driver to torch her house, maybe taking her out at the same time. The driver, Kinsey, knows you father because they share the same bookie and probably see each other here and there at the different Indian casinos, etcetera. He recruits your father to buy the accelerant, to help start the fire, perhaps to look the other way until it's too late. I just learned tonight that the elaborate fire alarm system required by the insurance company was out of service. That takes codes and inside information. It's the piece of evidence most damning to Nelson Lingford."

"Then he is guilty."

"Looks like it. After the fire and your dad's death, Lingford severs day-to-day connections with the driver by seeming to fire him. What Lingford doesn't count on is Kinsey's inability to hold on to money, even an exceptionally large amount like that one. And his greed. Kinsey spends all his loot and begins to wonder about your dad's share. Katie has disappeared, but he knows what she looks like, and eventually, maybe when he saw Katie with Lingford on the day of the hit-and-run, he puts Caroline Mays and Katie Fields together."

"Wouldn't he tell Lingford?"

"I don't think so. I think he'd try finding your dad's share of the fire money first."

"So you don't think he tried to run Katie over?"

"No. I think that was Lingford. Perhaps he borrowed a van from an associate. We checked rental records so we know he didn't get one that way. I think Katie must have tipped her hand when they spoke. Maybe she mentioned Kinsey by name."

"But Irene hadn't given her Kinsey's name yet."

"She could have said something else damning. Or Lingford may have had her investigated and learned Caroline's true identify."

Tess winced and he touched her hand. "Sorry. Bad phrasing. Once Lingford's charged with a few felonies and murder one, he might get talkative."

"So then Lingford decided to silence Kinsey?"

"Either that or Kinsey decided to try to shake down Lingford for additional cash and Nelson decided to cut his loses."

"Blackmail."

He grabbed her hands. "At any rate, once they've arrested Lingford, you'll be safe. Katie will be safe."

She looked twice as worn-out as the day before. Nodding at the shoe box on her lap, he said, "You've had a busy night."

"You don't know the half of it. There are a couple of bullet holes in your car. I was standing on the sidewalk in front of Lingford's building when someone shot at me."

"Shot at you?" He looked stunned. "I don't understand—"

"I don't, either. Obviously, I got away. I came here and then I couldn't sleep so I went to Katie's garage and then her apartment. I want to go through the notebook. I know I missed something in there. I came back here to do it but fell asleep."

"It doesn't matter," he said, bringing one of her hands to his lips and kissing it. "I'll call the shooting in to headquarters. Maybe Lingford thought he could silence you."

"He did know I would be at his office," she admitted. "We sort of had a date. I wanted to get a look at that trophy." Ryan's face clouded over and she added, "Still, I don't know."

"You don't know what?"

"I've met him a couple of times now, and though he's slick and probably dishonest, he doesn't strike me as stupid."

He stared into her eyes. "What's your point?"

"I don't think Lingford would drive around an intended victim's neighborhood in a distinctive car just minutes before or after strangling him. I don't think he'd use his own meds to knock someone out. I don't think he'd leave fingerprints on a glass. The murder scene looked staged to me. And why try to shoot me? Something is wrong."

He stood abruptly. "I keep forgetting," he said, holding up a finger, "that you're a detective. I keep thinking you're a veterinarian."

She gazed up at him. "Don't you have even the slightest feeling that you're being manipulated?"

"By you? Sometimes."

"Not by me. By someone else. Vince Desota for instance. Where does he fit into all this?"

"Maybe if you were more familiar with how stupid murderers can be, you wouldn't be so skeptical. People act out of desperation."

"Nelson Lingford? If a man like him hires an arsonist, why in the world wouldn't he hire a murderer?"

"Loose ends," Ryan said. "Maybe Lingford just got tired of other people botching up his plans."

"I don't like it," she insisted.

"Let me ask you this, Tess. Why couldn't you sleep last night? What was scarier to you than being outside with someone shooting at you? My place, that's what. Sitting here, waiting for me was more frightening to you than risking your neck. Needing me is scarier to you than taking a bullet."

She stared at him without answering.

The pager on his belt went off, its innocent little beep making both of them jump. Excusing himself, he walked into the bedroom and returned Sanchez's call. The conversation was brief but satisfying. As he came back into the living room, he spotted the papers sitting beside the computer and remembered the photos he'd printed off Katie's cell phone. He'd planned on using them as a sort of peace offering and had forgotten all about them. They might still come in handy.

Tess had opened the shoe box and taken out her father's notebook which she was thumbing through with her brow furrowed in concentration. "Names," she mumbled. "Oh, I see. Now I remember."

"Remember what?" he said.

"Why Irene's name sounded familiar when she mentioned it. My father made a record of the musicians he'd played with over the years. One of the first was a guy by the name of I. Woodall. That must be Irene's late husband, Ian Woodall. It's been bugging me. I thought it might be something, but it's not." She put the notebook back in the shoe box and added, "Who paged you?"

Her blue eyes were not only troubled and tired, they were wary. She'd been acting standoffish ever since he got home. For a second his step faltered.

Maybe it was his imagination.

"Sanchez." He swallowed deeply but remained standing. "Lingford allowed them to search his house, the arrogant bastard, but once they found his prescription for sleeping pills he rescinded permission and clammed up. Unfortunately for him, however, they'd already found a pair of muddy shoes in his garage, hidden under a tarp and guess what kind of bumper sticker he has?"

"A California windsurfing club."

"Give the lady a cigar. They'll compare

the mud on the shoes and in the car with the mud outside Kinsey's place and do all the other hocus-pocus lab stuff, and you watch, Lingford will start talking. I told them to look for any guns he has and take them along for testing. I assume there's a bullet lurking in my car somewhere? Case closed."

"Hmm," she said.

He frowned. He recalled the photos and handed them to her. They were eight-by-ten blowups, a little fuzzy, but not bad. There were ten of them and he watched as she shuffled through them, pausing at the one of Katie and her father at the picnic.

"You printed these off Katie's phone?"

"Yeah. There was never an opportunity before to give them to you. I guess now that you've seen all your sister's photos, these don't mean as much—"

"No, these are special, these are the ones she cared enough to save on her phone. The picture gallery got erased. Did you do it?"

"I guess I might have done it inadvertently," he said. He studied her a second longer, then lowered his voice. "Okay, out with it. What's going on?"

"I told you, I just have a feeling—"

"Not with the case and its resolution. Not with Katie or your father. What's wrong with us?"

She met his gaze straight on. "It's going too fast," she said bluntly.

"Too fast. As in lovemaking—"

"As in everything. I didn't know you existed a week ago. I didn't know anyone here existed a week ago." She put aside the notebook and the papers and stood up, hugging herself.

"We'll slow it down," he said. "We'll fly between here and San Francisco. We'll date. We'll take our time and get to know each other the way normal people do."

"What happened with your brother?"

Just like that she brought up Peter. Did his relationship with her hinge on his sharing the details of the major tragedy of his life?

Maybe it did. But could he talk about it at the drop of a hat after years of keeping it inside?

He stood there in the bright light of his apartment, staring at the woman he suspected he loved. Did he have a choice?

"Never mind," she said, rubbing her temples. "I'm sorry, that was cruel. It just goes to show how little you and I know about each other. I can be impatient and thoughtless. You have deep, dark secrets. Who knows what else. And—"

"Just stop," he said, taking a deep breath. Halting at first, his words gained momentum as he continued. "It's really pretty easy. I let him down. He was eighteen years old and called me for help. But I was in the police academy, a big test was coming up the next morning, one I couldn't miss and still graduate on schedule. I didn't go when he begged me. And by noon the next day he was dead of a drug overdose and it was too late. That's the story. It's not big and it's not complicated or unexpected or even unusual in today's world, but it's the shame of my life and now you know. You're the only one who knows."

"Your parents?"

"I never told them about the call."

"Because you thought they would blame you?"

"Because I knew they would forgive me," he said, his voice cracking. He took a deep breath and added, "It wasn't the first time Peter had called for help. I'd rushed to his aid many times before. He'd messed up every opportunity he had to straighten out. He'd worn out all the other members of our family. I was the only one left he could turn to. But that night he needed help. He reached out, and I failed him."

She put her arms around him. "You know how illogical this is, don't you?" she whispered close to his ear.

Her arms felt like a fragile grasp of heaven, an angel's touch. He shook inside as he said, "I guess."

She held him away and peered into his eyes. "You know you couldn't have anticipated your brother's death. You know he was hell-bound for a fall despite the efforts of everyone who loved him? How were you to anticipate this was his last chance, your last chance? And even if you'd put your life on hold and rushed to his aid, there would likely have been another time and another until he managed to kill himself or drive you away or finally take control and conquer his addiction. You know all this, don't you?"

Shocked by the tears he could feel burning behind his nose, he tried to move away.

But she wouldn't let him. Searching his eyes with hers, she finally said in a voice so tender it shook him, "Oh, baby."

It was the last straw, that affectionate word

uttered in that compassionate way. She pulled him to her. His chest heaved. The next thing he knew, he'd buried his head against her neck, buried himself in her and he was doing the unthinkable: crying.

There was no pretty way to end such a breakdown, and once the worst was over, he dreaded facing her, ashamed of himself because he figured he'd brought this on himself by never dealing with reality, always pushing it away. He found a tissue and took care of the damage from the waterworks, hands shaky at first, growing steadier as he moderated his breathing.

The next step would be talking to his parents. They'd probably spent a decade wondering why they lost two sons instead of one the day Peter died, because Ryan suspected his reluctance to talk about Peter had been as hard on them as it had been on him.

And yet...there were still all these vague issues floating around. He'd assumed that once the brains behind Tess's father's death was found, once the person responsible for Katie's hit-and-run was uncovered, once the man who attacked Tess had been outwitted, they would move ahead.

He chanced a look at her. She said, "Thank you."

He knew what she meant and so he nodded. It seemed silly to thank her in return, but the truth was he did feel fifty pounds lighter.

"It explains why you took Katie's situation so hard."

"I guess it does," he said. Moving his hand back and forth between them, he added, "But I don't see what it has to do with this thing between us."

"It explains why you protect yourself. It's as though you're finally ready to forgive yourself and step out of the dark, safe place you've created. I'm afraid, I'm terrified it's because of me, and I don't know, it's all so fast, there's something missing with this case and Katie—"

She stopped talking abruptly as tears brightened her eyes and slid down her cheeks.

He couldn't have been more shocked if she'd sprouted wings and flown through the window. It was his turn to reach for her, but she turned away, and suddenly he understood.

"You're afraid I care more for you than you do for me. You're afraid if you change your mind, I'll wallow in misery forever," he said. "Like I did with my brother."

She turned back to him and nodded.

He didn't know what to say. He didn't know if he was the only crazy one in the room or not. Why was she worrying about this? He knew no relationship came with a guarantee. He said, "So you don't even want to try?" and was stunned with the hurt he heard in his voice. As a shining example of manliness, he was a big flop.

"I don't know what I want," she said. "It's just—"

"There's more?"

She blinked a couple of times as though trying to decide if she wanted to add anything and finally said, "All you care about is finding out who's guilty."

"Isn't that the bottom line?"

"No. The bottom line for me is more complicated. What was my father doing at the Lingford house?"

"Starting a fire."

"Has anyone proven that?"

"The fuel can, the receipt—"

"Could have all been planted."

"The wild-goose chase he sent me on. The graft that came out later. The money, for heaven's sake, Tess," he added, his voice rising. "The money *you* found!"

"I'm still not convinced," she said, her stubbornness reaching new and profound heights. "I think you're settling on an answer too soon, that you want this to be over so it's over."

Incredulous, he stared at her. "Now you're questioning my ethics as a cop?"

"I—"

"You suddenly know more than all the police in New Harbor, is that it?" he added. "More than Sanchez, more than Donovan and certainly a hell of a lot more than me."

She didn't move.

"Fine," he said. "Go ask all the questions you want. Be Tess Mays or Katie Fields or Caroline Mays or Wonder Woman if you want. Nelson Lingford is in custody, he can't hurt you or his stepmother, and Kinsey is dead, so knock yourself out."

He threw up his hands.

She picked up the shoe box, the notebook and the photos and nodded curtly. He didn't turn as she gathered the rest of her belongings or when he heard a thunk on the table and figured she'd just returned his car keys. He didn't turn until he heard the door shut and then he moved to the window, angling to see the sidewalk, watching until at last he had to accept she'd walked off in the other direction.

He kicked the ottoman and swore.

Chapter Twelve

Tess walked the few blocks to the hospital. She'd left the crutches and the pseudo cast at Ryan's place.

She wouldn't think about Ryan. Shame or regret or maybe both gnawed away in the deepest pit of her stomach. She'd allowed things to get out of hand. But how could she give up when Katie still depended on her to uncover the truth that would salvage their father's name?

Is that the whole reason or are you hiding behind Katie's needs to mask your own?

How could she *need* a man she'd known such a short time, when the game plan was and always had been that she should never need a man at all?

Katie's phone rang a block from the hospital. Tess had to juggle the pictures Ryan had given her to dig the phone out of a pocket.

"Caroline, dear? It's Madeline," came a soft voice.

It wasn't Ryan, it might never be Ryan again. She'd pushed him into leaving her. How clever! Now she didn't have to leave him, or worse, wait for the day when he decided he'd had enough and rode off into the sunset, her heart in his back pocket.

She was an emotional coward—just like her mother....

And heaven help her, she was weak with relief that this call wasn't Ryan. She couldn't talk to him. She wouldn't know what to say.

"Have you heard? They've arrested Nelson!"

"I just heard," Tess said, a new crop of tears rolling down her cheeks, tears that had nothing to do with Nelson.

"I'm devastated," Madeline cried. "The police are saying Nelson killed a man. They're saying he was behind my fire! I can't bear to stay here. I'm on my way to a friend's house in Portland. I'm dropping off all the photos at Irene's place first. She said I could, that Georges will be there to let me in but it's Sunday and he has plans and has to leave right away. Will you meet me? Will you wait for Irene? She's with Tabitha but she'll be along soon."

"Okay," Tess said woodenly. She owed Madeline and Irene an explanation. Might as well get it over with. "I have to stop by and visit...a friend first," Tess said, eyeing the photo Ryan had printed, the one of Tabitha in her party hat. The one Katie took the day she was hit by a white van. The young girl smiling, cake crumbs on her chin, a pink party hat perched on her head, art in the background. She could give the photo to Irene to give to Tabitha. She could say goodbye.

There was a moment of silence before Madeline added, "Caroline? Is everything okay?"

"Everything is fine," Tess said.

"Okay. The store is on Broadway—100 Broadway Ave."

Tess resumed walking to the hospital. She found Katie as she always found her, in bed, out like a light. However, many of her tubes had been removed and the head bandages modified, so that now Tess could see the beginnings of light roots at her sister's hairline.

She leaned close and whispered, "I have

to tell you some bad news about Dad. Wake up, please."

But it wasn't that easy, and Tess had known it wouldn't be. She kissed her sister's hand. Would they ever look into each other's eyes?

RYAN PACED HIS LIVING ROOM for a while before calling Sanchez again. He asked a few questions and listened to a few answers, splashed his face with cold water and left the apartment. Ten minutes later he was at the precinct.

Nelson Lingford had started talking again. He swore he had nothing to do with Kinsey's death. Surprise. He swore he didn't know how his muddy shoes got under the tarp, but he did admit he'd driven to Kinsey's neighborhood. He said Kinsey had called him and he'd gone, but something about the call sounded fishy, so in the end he didn't stop.

The mud on his boots suggested otherwise.

No recently fired gun in his possession, though. That fact really bothered Ryan, though it was easy to get rid of an unwanted weapon when you lived close to a great big ocean. Still, the guy was guilty. Everyone knew it.

Except Tess.

And she was out there somewhere, bumbling along, asking questions, snooping, refusing to face reality and the truth. Alone. Or maybe not alone. If Nelson didn't try to kill her, was there someone else?

Should he be worried about her?

That depended. Was he one hundred percent sure Nelson Lingford was responsible for every single thing that happened? Him and Kinsey? If so, then she was safe.

If there was even a shred of doubt, she wasn't safe.

Her safety was his priority.

But she doesn't want you around, his pride whispered.

"Ryan? You okay?"

Ryan looked up to find Sanchez staring at him.

"I'm going to go talk to that neighbor," Ryan said. "The one with the rug."

"Go for it," Sanchez said.

Ryan assembled a few photographs and left the office. He stopped by Katie's building first. Once again he knocked on doors, showing pictures to anyone who answered, asking anyone if they'd seen Lingford or Kinsey.

He even tried the grouch's door and was surprised when the old guy actually took a moment to look at the pictures. He shook his head no, closed the door and then opened it again. A dog peeked from behind his leg. "This to help the little redhead at the end of the hall?" he demanded.

"Yes, it is. Have you recalled seeing one of these men?"

"What I seen was a woman who don't belong here. I seen her outside in a van."

Surprised by this unexplained cooperation, Ryan asked a slew of questions.

"I seen her twice," the old guy answered. "A few days ago and again yesterday. I don't know what she looked like. Gray hair, maybe white, maybe blond, hard to tell in the rain but she was wearing a blue scarf, tied at the neck. Light-colored van. Morning one time, afternoon the other. Sitting in the driver's seat."

Ryan didn't know what, if anything, the old guy's observations meant. The woman in the van could be someone's ex-wife, part of a new car pool or a dozen other things. He questioned him further about the scarf—was it blue-and-white striped? The old man couldn't recall. He slammed his door once his natural surliness resurfaced.

So, what did this mean? The only women involved in the case were Irene Woodall and Madeline Lingford. Was it possible Madeline wasn't as crippled as everyone thought? That she was hell-bent on protecting her stepson? Was it possible Irene was jealous of what she considered her paintings?

He drove to Kinsey's neighborhood next and walked up the drive of the rug beater's house. The woman who answered the door seemed excited to review details, the kind of neighbor who minds everyone's business, half frightened by the idea of a murder so close by, half titillated.

"I want to know about the man you saw walking along the street yesterday, the one you told the officer who interviewed you last night was a stranger."

"Isn't it terrible? To think that man was murdered two doors down in the middle of the day!"

"I know, it's terrible. Now, about the man you waved to?"

"A total stranger. I know who lives on this block and the one over and the one over from that. I know most everybody, and I'd never seen this person before and I would have remembered because of the blue and white striped scarf and because he was, well, you know…"

"What do you mean?"

She shrugged plump shoulders and looked embarrassed. "He was one of *them*."

"Them? Mrs. Pilsner, one of whom?"

"One of those men who want to be a woman."

Marcel? Doyle? *What?* What did either man have to do with anything? Doyle maybe, in some convoluted way, but Doyle a cross-dresser? "How do you know?" he asked.

She talked in circles for a moment before finally saying, "So I knew at once that it was a man trying to be a woman dressed up like a man."

Pretty sure he'd missed something, he said, "And why couldn't it have been a woman dressed like a man?"

She shrugged. "That's too simple, isn't it?"

Hell, he didn't know. Nothing was simple. He showed her the pictures he'd shown Katie's neighbor and she didn't recognize anyone but Nelson Lingford, whom she admitted having seen pictures of in the newspaper over the years. He could have been the walker, but she wasn't sure.

What he needed were pictures of Irene and Madeline. He'd swing back by the station and see if Donovan had any.

He had another thought and took out his cell phone, punching in Katie's number, his thoughts tumbling over one another as he waited for Tess to answer. It switched to voice mail. He called the hospital and learned Tess had left some time before.

He started off down the street, knocking on doors, showing pictures, growing increasingly uneasy. Who was this mystery woman? Was she important or an unimportant tangent?

And he thought of Tess. Where was she? Would he ever see her again?

IRENE'S STORE WAS CALLED Broadway Art. Smaller letters below the gold leaf proclaimed: Sales, Acquisition, Custom Framing. The front window housed a display of landscapes.

The sign on the door said the store was closed, but Tess tried the handle and knocked gently on the glass. The door opened, and she let herself in.

The store itself was larger than it appeared from the street and filled with art. Statues perched on pedestals, paintings hung on fiber-coated walls, hand-blown glass and other objets d'art each with its own spotlight and enough space around it to show it at maximum advantage. Tess saw a few price tags and almost choked.

Irene peeked out of a room in the back. "Come on back. I plugged in the coffeemaker."

She disappeared as Tess made her way through the gallery to the back room. On the walk over from the hospital, she'd tried to decide how best to tell both women the truth about her identity. Part of her wished she'd worn the glasses and the crutches and delayed this moment.

After all, it wasn't as though she lived in New Harbor. She'd come here for Katie, but once Katie recovered, she might like to move to San Francisco. Tess had an extra room and a little money put away. She could give it to Katie to go to school, to start over somewhere new, somewhere different, somewhere a long way away from Ryan Hill.

And yet it went against her nature to keep this kind of secret. When Nelson Lingford went to trial, some of this would come out, and it would be better if the two older women heard the truth from her.

The back room was obviously the heart of Irene's business. Framing equipment, rolls of canvas and tools covered several workbenches. The boxes of Madeline's photographs occupied a corner of the closest worktable.

There were two doors on the back wall, a large freight door and a smaller door that currently stood open. A light-gray van was parked directly outside right next to Irene's black sedan.

Tess had counted fifteen vans on her walk to the store. They were everywhere. How could a legally blind man tell the difference between light gray or white or silver or probably pale yellow or light blue. It had been raining. Vans were a dime a dozen.

Irene closed and locked the small door. "Tabitha wasn't well enough to spend much time with me this morning, so I came into work and sent Georges home," she said. "You just missed Madeline. She was in a hurry. I told her you and I would make a window display to honor the collection." She looked at Tess more closely and added, "Good heavens! Where are your crutches and cast?"

"I'm better," Tess said as the first few notes of "Für Elise" announced a call.

"And your glasses?" Irene said, eyebrows raised. "Your eyesight is better, too?"

"Yes," Tess said simply, checking the display on Katie's cell phone.

Ryan. A rush of excitement was followed by doubt. Was it wise to give him false hope? What could she say, what should she say? She turned the phone off and set it on the workbench.

"Problem?" Irene said.

"No. Just my…cousin."

"He's very devoted."

"I just can't talk to him right now," Tess said.

Irene leaned against the worktable, linking her arms across her chest and said, "That man isn't you cousin. I'm not so old I don't remember how it is when a man looks at you the way this man does. Did you have a fight?"

"Not all love stories end in a perfect marriage," Tess said softly.

Irene flashed her a quick, appraising look. "I never said I had a perfect marriage," she said.

Tess picked up one of the photos of the lost art and mumbled, "I'm sorry. I guess I assumed."

"Ian was a professional musician so he traveled a great deal. He also played in a small local ensemble, in fact, you're not going to believe this, but he played in the same little group that the cop accused of starting Madeline's house fire played in. Years ago, of course. Ian played the violin."

Tess already knew this. "He sounds great," she mumbled as she opened the box of photos and took out a stack. She paused over a Monet, a painting of a child on a bench. She'd seen the photo before. That's right, she'd seen it at Madeline's house.

As it so happened, the photo of the painting depicting a dog running through the poppies, the painting Madeline had claimed her favorite, sat right next to the Monet. The difference in the quality was so stunning it was no wonder Irene found Madeline's lack of sophistication when it came to art humorous.

"But Ian, bless his heart, wasn't the true love of my life," Irene said.

Tess glanced up. Irene had lifted the stack of photos Ryan had printed out. "Doesn't Tabitha look happy in this picture?" she said, handing the photo of her daughter over to Tess. "Caroline, may I borrow your phone?"

Tess glanced at the phone sitting on the workbench.

Irene said, "I need a cell phone for this call and mine is in my car."

Tess handed over Katie's phone. Something intangible in the atmosphere of the workroom had changed. Something was wrong. Tess cast about wildly for an explanation as Irene text-messaged on Katie's phone.

"Actually," Irene said as she finished her task and clicked off the phone, "I was madly in love with Theo Lingford."

Tess blinked a couple of times.

"Are you shocked? Do you think your generation is the first to have affairs?"

"No," Tess said. What shocked her was Irene telling her about it. What was the point? Anxious to avoid Irene's probing stare and bizarre confession, she glanced down at Tabitha's photo again.

And this time she finally saw what she should have seen from the beginning. She all but did a double take. Her breath caught short of a gasp.

Behind Tabitha Woodall's shoulder was a painting, more visible now because of the enlargement. Tess finally recognized it: the child on a bench, a Monet, small and perfect.

What was a painting supposedly destroyed in a fire months before doing in a picture taken only days ago? Had Katie grasped the significance right away? Had she tried to reach Ryan to tell him about this and not the trophy in Nelson Lingford's office?

She could picture it. The innocent photo of Tabitha, pretty much ignored until Katie arrived at Nelson's office. Scrolling through the photos to show him the image she'd just taken of his silly trophy, spying that tiny little painting behind Tabitha, sudden comprehension, leaving abruptly to call Ryan in private...

Irene said, "Madeline is wrong, you know. The little Renoir wasn't Theo's favorite. Monet's painting of the child on the bench was his favorite. We bought it on a trip to Paris. He said it reminded him of his daughter, or of what she could have been if she hadn't been born...different."

Tess's gaze flew to Irene as flickers of understanding fought against denial. "Theo Lingford was Tabitha's father?"

Irene nodded.

"Does Madeline know?"

"Madeline isn't the brightest bulb in the pack," Irene said. "I don't believe she ever cottoned on to what was going on right under her nose. She didn't even realize I orchestrated her sudden flight from town today, that it was I who suggested she come here, that she call you. Silly, silly, woman."

When did Katie's trouble start? After the party. After Katie took Tabitha's picture. The witness of the hit-and-run stated the driver of the van approached Katie as she lay on the sidewalk. Looking to help or looking for an object, a cell phone, perhaps? Scared away, had the driver come back to search Katie's apartment? The phone would have been in police custody by then. Then Tess showed up looking and acting like Katie, still snooping, still wielding the phone, oblivious to the importance of Tabitha's photo on that phone. The pictures had been erased—she'd assumed by Ryan, maybe Nelson—but actually by Irene. Then she'd brought a hard-print photo right to Irene's store and shoved it under her nose.

Tess wondered what had Nelson been accused of that Irene couldn't have done: she'd already admitted she knew Tess's father, probably heard rumors from her husband about his gambling problems, so there was that connection; she knew about the alarm system in the house; knowing Madeline for years undoubtedly meant she also knew Madeline's driver, the late Jim Kinsey, so there was another connection. She gave out Kinsey's name, and then before anyone could talk to him, he was strangled by someone he trusted enough to have a drink with, someone clever enough to plant Nelson's muddy shoes in his own garage, swipe glasses with his fingerprints from his den, steal a few of his sleeping tablets. Someone intimate with the family.

All to cover up the theft of one painting?

Tess met Irene's gaze again, and she knew her suppositions were right on the money. Trouble was, she could tell Irene knew she knew.

"Let's drop the charade," Irene said. "It wasn't until you came to Tabitha's party that I was sure you were Matt's daughter, pretending to be someone else, prying, asking questions. And then Tabitha had one of her tantrums. In the confusion, the drapery over the Monet got pushed aside. While I was in the kitchen preparing her medication, you took matters into your own hands and quieted Tabitha with the promise of a photo of her wearing her new kitty necklace. As soon as I came back in the room and saw that curtain thrust aside, I suspected what else you might have caught on that stupid phone."

"You didn't know for sure? You ran...me... down but you didn't know?"

"I couldn't take the chance. I should have vaulted that painting like the others, but it was Theo's favorite. It was my link to him. Anyway, I had to stop you before you realized what you'd done."

"So you tried to shoot me last night—"

"Shoot you? Why would I shoot you until I made sure you hadn't told anyone what you suspected?"

There was a glint of determination in Irene's eyes. Taking a step toward the storeroom door, Tess said, "My cousin knows—"

"Your *cousin,* detective Ryan Hill, is on his way," Irene said. "He's who I text messaged. He should be here any moment. There'll be a lover's quarrel. Perhaps it will revolve around your father's fifty grand, the money Kinsey was trying to get you to hand over before I killed him, the greedy bastard. Maybe you want it for yourself and Ryan refuses to give it to you. You'll grab my gun and shoot Ryan Hill, he'll grab his and shoot you, the ruckus will start a fire—look at the solvents on my shelves, turpentine is so volatile!—my shop will be destroyed. I'll barely escape."

Tess shook her head but her heart was beating like the wings of a hummingbird. "He won't come," she said.

Irene raised her hand. She was holding a revolver, pointing it straight at Tess's forehead, a gun way too big for the woman's slender hand. It looked to Tess's inexperienced eye like Kinsey's gun. Eventually she and Ryan would be linked back to Kinsey and his death and then to her father and then the Lingford fire. Eventually Katie would wake up to a new nightmare.

Her long-lost sister, dead. Claimed to be a criminal.

Ryan dead.

No! Not Ryan.

She had to do something.

RYAN TRIED THE HANDLE on the front door and was surprised when it turned in his hand. Not as surprised as when he'd received Tess's message asking him to meet her here, but surprised.

Drawing his gun, he closed the door behind him and moved through the darkened store. "Honey? Where are you? Answer me."

He heard a noise in the workroom and entered the space to find Tess standing next to Irene Woodall. After a cursory look at Tess, who was as white and stiff as a newly stretched canvas, he focused on Irene Woodall. After all, she was the one with the gun; she was undoubtedly the one who had summoned him.

"Looks like a standoff," he said.

"It depends on how much you think of this girl," Irene said.

"I think the world of her." He could hear a faint noise at the door in the back of the room. The trick was to get Tess out of harm's way. His eyes darting to Tess's face, he added, "In fact, I love her."

There was a millisecond where Tess's gaze met his, and despite their predicament he felt a flicker of hope. Was it possible she loved him, too?

"It's a shame she has to kill you," Irene said, and without further warning, fired. Tess had used the moment of inattention to pull on Irene's arm, and the shot went wild. The two women crashed to the floor as Sanchez broke down the back door. Ryan ran to help

Tess. Another shot. He pulled Tess away and kicked the gun out of Irene's hand. Sanchez subdued the older woman as Ryan turned back to Tess.

A bloody stain spread across her white sweater.

She began to fall in slow motion, her gaze connected to his. He grabbed her, cradling her as she sank to the floor. "Call an ambulance!" he yelled, his insides choking, his heart crying, No, no!

Someone handed him a clean square of cloth and he held it against Tess's chest. "Stay with me," he said, looking down at her face. "Tess, stay with me, my love."

"Stay with you," she repeated, her voice faint, fading away...gone.

GROGGY AND CONFUSED, Tess peered at her surroundings, trying to make sense of what she saw.

A hospital room. Katie's room? No Katie, though.

A warm hand grasped hers and she turned her head.

"Ryan," she croaked.

He looked down at her with his gray eyes, a look of concern gradually giving way to relief. "I'm here," he said. "Better, you're here."

"How long—"

"It's been almost a week. You were hurt so badly. There was an emergency operation, then you had a fever. I began to worry you might never come back to me, Tess Mays."

Tears glittered in his eyes.

"I love you," she said. "I *need* you. I shouldn't have tried not to need you. It was stupid."

"Shh," he said, leaning over and kissing her forehead. "I love you, too," he whispered against her skin. "I need you, too. Needing each other is a good thing. You'll marry me, of course."

"Of course," she mumbled. "Of course."

A few moments later, when she awoke again, he told her about Irene. Offered a deal that would spare her life, she'd been singing like a canary. Tess already knew most of what Ryan told her. What she didn't know was that soon after Theo Lingford died, Irene began stealing paintings and replacing them with fakes she'd procured halfway around the world. "Fabulous fakes," she called them, "brilliant reproductions." One at a time she walked off with a dozen of the smaller canvases. No one noticed. Madeline peered at them every single day and never noticed a thing. It wasn't until Madeline insisted on donating the collection that Irene panicked. Donation meant authentication and that meant discovery, exposure, shame, prosecution. She delayed with the photo ploy and when Georges caught on to what she'd done and tried his hand at a little blackmailing, she killed him.

"Georges! Dead?"

"That's why he was never around. We found his body in her chest freezer, upstairs from the gallery. He's been dead for weeks. Anyway, she decided she would have to destroy the forged paintings. She hired your father who subsequently hired Kinsey. Your father had a change of heart when he realized Madeline Lingford hadn't left the house. He tried to stop Kinsey, who punched him out and left him to burn to death. The subsequent blaze destroyed most of the collection, not just the forgeries. It was this Irene was most upset about. Not your dad's death or Georges' and Kinsey's murders or the trouble she'd caused Madeline and Nelson Lingford. Just the art."

"After Katie took the photo of Tabitha,

Irene realized she had to act fast," Tess said, breathing shallowly as the pain in her chest increased. "She had to get the phone and erase that photo before Katie realized what else was in the picture."

"That's right. She didn't know Katie had seen an article in the newspaper and almost at once recognized what she had. Irene ran over Katie then searched her apartment the first time. Then she told Kinsey who Caroline Mays really was and hired him to kill Katie—you—but Kinsey got greedy. He wanted the money before he did the killing. Irene realized he needed to go, too. Might as well take out two birds with one stone and set the blame firmly on Nelson. She baited Nelson to go to the neighborhood, and framed him for Kinsey's murder. She was the woman dressed up like a man, using Nelson's overcoat and scarf. I realized it about two minutes before Irene used your cell phone to send for me. She was the only possibility."

"How did you know it wasn't me?"

He smiled. "I knew you were too stubborn to call me first. You wouldn't even answer my call. That's why I asked Sanchez for backup."

"But the paintings," Tess said, feeling slightly more alert. The price of better awareness, she was discovering, was pain. Her chest throbbed. "What could she do with the paintings?" she asked, her voice catching. "They'd be impossible to sell, wouldn't they?"

"She sold them to a place overseas that vaults them for twenty years. Of course, she got only a fraction of their true value, but her needs weren't huge and she took only the best of the best. She just wanted enough to keep her daughter comfortable. She knew Tabitha and she would most likely be dead within twenty years, and it wouldn't matter when the paintings started showing up again. The FBI and Interpol have been notified. In the end, hopefully some or most will be recovered."

"Tabitha Woodall is Theo Lingford's daughter," Tess whispered, pain prowling through her body like a panther on the loose.

"She hasn't told anyone else that piece of information," Ryan said, smoothing her hair away from her face, his hand warm and soothing. She vaguely recalled him holding her as the ambulance wailed in the distance. The feeling of safety, of refuge...of home.

"Irene told me Tabitha's father had provided for her. Not her husband. Tabitha's father. She must have meant Theo Lingford."

"I think she figured that art was hers to do with as she pleased," he said. He added, "You look miserable. I'm calling for a nurse."

Tess closed her eyes. What would have happened if Irene had told Madeline the truth about Tabitha? Maybe Madeline, a down-to-earth woman, would have offered to help Irene. Surely Irene could have proven paternity and sued for half of Theo Lingford's estate if money was her only goal.

But perhaps it went deeper than that. Perhaps she liked putting something over on Madeline, perhaps she felt entitled to manipulate the world to her own ends.

"She said she didn't shoot at me," Tess said softly.

"That honor goes to Vince Desota. He thought you were Nelson's girlfriend. He thought if he killed you, then Nelson would suffer, and all Vince wants is for Nelson to suffer like he has. That's why he sent the charcoal briquettes, to taunt Nelson about the fire, trying to scare him into thinking his house was going to go up in flames next. Vince actually came forward and confessed his shooting spree. I think some time in jail will do him good."

"Hmm…" Tess's eyes flew open. "Oh, my gosh, my mother. Ryan, what about my mother? Did she return my calls, have you heard from her—"

Ryan looked over her bed toward the door. "Good timing," he said to someone standing there. Looking back at Tess, he added, "She'll bring you up to speed."

Tess turned her head slowly, expecting to see her mother. She found herself looking at herself.

"Katie?"

Katie, red hair tamed into a ponytail, expression incredulous, limped toward the bed.

"Ryan tells me you've been having quite the adventure," she said softly, her eyes full of wonder. She reached out a hand and gently gripped Tess's hand.

"Hello," Tess murmured, her heart swelling.

"I heard you while I was sleeping," Katie whispered. "I heard you inside my head, urging me to wake up."

The two sisters stared at each other, tears

sliding down their identical cheeks. Finally Tess said, "I have to tell you about Dad."

Katie shook her head. "Ryan already told me. I wish you could have known him. He was weak, but he wasn't evil. He wouldn't kill someone. He died trying to save Madeline Lingford."

"I know," Tess said.

"But I have to tell you about Mom."

A tremor of alarm swept through Tess. A nurse bustled in with a tray. Tess focused on Katie. "Has she called?"

"No, and that stepson of hers won't talk to me. Someone has to go to Alaska and find out what's going on, Tess. You can't. That leaves me."

Tess started to argue, but as the nurse emptied a shot into her IV and drugs raced through her system, she accepted the unavoidable wisdom of Katie's decision.

Tess couldn't go, not now, not for a while.

Their mother was missing. It was Katie's turn.

She looked at Ryan, who raised her hand to his lips and kissed her fingers, his eyes full of promises she knew he would keep.

Promises she wanted...and needed...him to keep. Promises she ached to return.

She wasn't an emotional coward after all.
How about that?
And then she fell asleep.

* * * * *

Be sure to pick up Katie Fields's story,
DUPLICATE DAUGHTER,
in July 2006
only from Harlequin Intrigue!

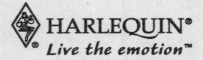

HARLEQUIN®
INTRIGUE®

WE'LL LEAVE YOU BREATHLESS!

If you've been looking for thrilling tales of contemporary passion and sensuous love stories with taut, edge-of-the-seat suspense—then you'll love Harlequin Intrigue!

Every month, you'll meet six new heroes who are guaranteed to make your spine tingle and your pulse pound. With them you'll enter into the exciting world of Harlequin Intrigue— where your life is on the line and so is your heart!

THAT'S INTRIGUE—
ROMANTIC SUSPENSE
AT ITS BEST!

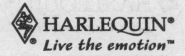

Live the emotion™

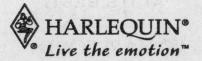

HARLEQUIN *Super*ROMANCE®

...there's more to the story!

Superromance.
A *big* satisfying read about unforgettable
characters. Each month we offer *six* very different
stories that range from family drama to adventure
and mystery, from highly emotional stories to
romantic comedies—and much more! Stories
about people you'll believe in and care about.
Stories too compelling to put down....

Our authors are among today's *best* romance
writers. You'll find familiar names and talented
newcomers. Many of them are award winners—
and you'll see why!

If you want the biggest and best
in romance fiction, you'll get it
from Superromance!

Emotional, Exciting, Unexpected...

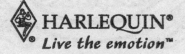
HARLEQUIN®
® *Live the emotion*™

 Harlequin Historicals®
Historical Romantic Adventure!

*From rugged lawmen and
valiant knights to defiant heiresses
and spirited frontierswomen,
Harlequin Historicals will
capture your imagination with
their dramatic scope, passion
and adventure.*

*Harlequin Historicals . . .
they're too good to miss!*